EXTRACT

'Why are you so jumpy?' Again, softly. 'Would you like me to go?' This time, he was propping up her chin with his index finger, so that even if she wanted to, she wouldn't be able to avert her face. She couldn't speak as her throat was getting dry. But she could manage a small shake of her head.

It was at this point that his head started slowly descending to hers. The anticipation was making her legs wobbly. He claimed her lips with gentle probing kisses. His kiss deepened and became hungrier.

'*Sean...*' Of its own volition, her mouth gasped out his name.

He frowned.

'Do you want me to stop, Gaby? If you do, you need to tell me now... because the things I want to do to you... I won't be able to stop myself later...' His voice was ragged with need.

She couldn't speak.

'*Gabriela...*' He was pleading with her to answer him.

Instead of speaking, she lifted her trembling hands to the bottom of his t-shirt and slowly started lifting it.

LET'S PLAY

Era Capoeira, Book 1

Shonel Jackson

The characters and events portrayed in this book are fictitious. Any similarity to real persons, living or dead, is coincidental and not intended by the author.

Paperback - ISBN: 978-1-7392521-1-3

This series is dedicated to my friend, my former acting colleague and my former Capoeira instructor, Seun Shote, a.k.a "Instrutor Sacrificio" / "Shy". You introduced me to this world which still lives in my heart and for that, and more, I will be forever grateful.

Rest In Power...

CONTENTS

REVIEWS

EMMA ASHLEY (27 NOVEMBER, 2022)

Let's Play is a brilliant romance novel with a great storyline and brilliant characters. The chemistry between the characters was believable and I would truly recommend it and read more by the author.

DALE (14TH NOVEMBER, 2022)

I enjoyed reading this book, this is the first time I've ever read anything from this author. But it's not going to be the last. I'm looking forward to seeing the entire series of Era Capoeira.

LET'S
PLAY
SHONEL JACKSON

CHAPTER 1

- ginga -

Gabriela had never seen anything like it before. She stood transfixed, looking through the small, open crack of the doorway at the room's lone occupant. It was the music that had drawn her to the door, but it was what she spied inside which had kept her rooted to the spot. Her brown eyes widened as she saw how his slow, sensual movements perfectly flowed with the rhythmic tones of the strangely enticing sounds coming from the music. His bare torso glistened with sweat. The muscles on his tall, shirtless frame, rippled with every twist, turn and undulation.

From the music, Gabriela could hear what she thought was a strange guitar-like strumming, some type of drum and maybe a tambourine. She wasn't sure, but it was so enthralling. She kept watching, as suddenly, it seemed like the mood in the room started to change. From slow and melodic, the music became more of a quick tempo, almost frenetic.

His movements followed suit. Every swing of his white trousers-clad legs and thrust of his arms somehow managed to tell a tale. Was it some kind of dance? If it was, Gabriela had never seen anything like it before. But if it wasn't, why did some of the movements look like... kicks? There was music playing too, so it must have been some kind of dance, right?

It got faster still. Now, these new movements were definitely kicks. They kind of reminded her now of some of those old martial arts movies she'd watched when she was growing up. Except, these kicks were almost... *sexy*!

Strange, that.

It looked like he was repeating one sequence of steps with his feet, but growing from that, were a whole array of steps, thrusts and kicks. Gabriela couldn't quite understand how these pugilistic movements still managed to look like a sensual dance.

Still, Gabriela remained glued to the sight of this tall, beautiful dancer, with his exposed chest, in his white trousers, with a blue, woven belt around his waist. The ends of the belt were so long that it swept the floor every time he went low.

So focused was she on him that she didn't

realise that the music had gone out. The man's movements did not waver. He didn't lose a step, though the guitar-like strum of the music had come to an end. Somehow, his movements became even more intense. The only sounds coming from the room now were that of his feet connecting with the wooden floor and the fast pace of his breathing.

How does he move like that?

She watched as he took his movements low to the floor, alternating having his full body weight on either of his feet and, or his hands. He manipulated himself in such a way that, to Gabriela, it evoked memories of watching a gymnast's floor routine at the Olympic Games or a B-boy or girl doing certain breakdancing tricks. Her breath caught in her chest as she watched him perform a movement which saw him launch one of his legs forward from a semi-crouched position and them magically, at least to her mind at that moment, end up back on both feet and seamlessly back into the repeated sequences of steps that she'd noted before. She was—

'Gabriela!'

A sudden, familiar, shrill voice rang out through the empty corridor. Though she knew who the owner of the voice was, the scene that had been unfolding in the room had so gripped her attention that the shout managed to startle her, and Gabriela let out an audible yelp.

The dancer's movement didn't falter at her noise, but for the first time, his gaze had swung over to the direction of the doorway. Without realising it, when Gabriela's name had been called out so suddenly, in her panic, she had automatically pushed the door open a lot wider. She was now fully visible. Two sets of eyes met, but on top of that, Gabriela's mouth was also wide open. She was incredibly embarrassed that she'd been caught snooping. The eyes that met hers, though, were not angry ones. Instead, they were playful. He smiled and inclined his head in acknowledgement of her presence as he continued with his mesmerising footwork.

'Gabriela, we're in *this* room.'

The shrill voice was that of her best friend Tanya, whom she turned to and waved at quickly before taking her attention back to the dancer. But he had already forgotten her and was once again fully engrossed in his movements. The only difference this time was that she was not hiding, trying to observe him covertly.

Reluctantly, Gabriela slowly pulled the door closed and took a deep, much-needed breath. Whatever that dance-thing was, Gabriela knew she wanted to try it. It looked a lot more interesting than the Pilates class she'd let Tanya talk her into doing tonight. Tanya had been coming here to this Sports Centre to take Pilates for a few months, but this was Gabriela's first time. She turned and walked towards Tanya, who stood by the neighbouring door. The only things going through Gabriela's mind as she walked were of the sensual music, his rippling muscles and those mesmerising eyes that had smiled at her.

As expected, the Pilates class was awful. It was quite possibly the most boring thing Gabriela had done in her life. She considered herself to be fairly athletic, so the movements were fairly easy to do. However, it felt monotonous and uninspiring. She watched the clock on the wall of the studio tick by, mind-numbingly slowly. Why she let Tanya talk her into this, she didn't know? To keep fit, she had leaned more towards salsa dancing, jogging and aerobics and even a bit of Zumba thrown in for good measure. *Fun*, Pilates was not.

After what seemed like forever, the class was over and the group started to file out of the door. Tanya had made her way over to the Pilates instructor and looked like she was engrossed in conversation. Gabriela grabbed her water bottle from the floor in the corner and walked over to Tanya, telling her that she'd meet her in the dressing room.

As she walked down the corridor, she could see that this time, it was not as empty as it was when she'd arrived earlier. It was filled with people in all manner of sportswear. This was a fairly new sports centre which looked pretty modern and came with the latest technical gadgets and equipment. It had a fully fitted gym on the other side of the building, and on this side, there was a long corridor of studios. Tanya said that there were classes for just about any sport here.

Among the different outfits that the people in the corridor were wearing, she could see three girls in identical ones, which looked familiar to her. They had on white t-shirts with a yellow, circular logo, bordered in black, on the front, upper left corner and long, white, straight-cut trousers with the same yellow logo on their upper left thigh area. Around their waists were abnormally long, colourful belts, with ends that hung down to around their knees. The belts were all different colours. One girl's belt was dark green, the other bright yellow and the third was a mix of both yellow and green.

How curious!

One thing she did know was that the dancer she'd been spying on earlier was wearing the same uniform, though his belt was blue and he was *sans* t-shirt. She was even more curious than she was earlier now that she saw the girls dressed like him.

In the dressing room, she had a quick shower, and within fifteen minutes, she was heading out the door again. Tanya was still not there. She must still be deep in conversation with the Pilates instructor. Gabriela had always thought that

Tanya could talk for England! Also, Tanya had confessed that she thought the instructor was cute, so Gabriela knew that she was in for a wait.

As she was walking back down the corridor, she pulled out her phone to check her messages. Her father had sent her a text, asking her to call him, and the others were from some other friends. She was so distracted by the phone that she didn't notice when a door opened just ahead of her. She also didn't know that the dancer from earlier was about to walk out of said door. He didn't have enough time to see her either, and as he turned, they slammed into each other. Gabriela's phone was sent flying up in the air and came crashing down to the floor. She barely noticed it. The only thing that registered was the hard, this time t-shirt covered, chest that she'd hit.

Was he made of stone?

Though she was tall, he was taller. She was a few inches shorter than he was. When they'd impacted, she was knocked off her balance and the man put his arms out and around her instinctively to stop her from falling. He also pulled her inwards towards him to steady her.

To steady herself, she put her hand out on his abdominals. Through his top, she could feel every wave of tightly toned muscle beneath.

'I'm so sorry,' she said as she lifted her face to his. They were inches apart.

When their eyes met, she was immediately

struck by how much more beautiful he was now that she was seeing him up close. Her breath caught in her throat. He was much too close. *She* was much too close. Her chest was rising and falling at a very rapid pace.

He didn't say a word. He just kept standing there holding her, now unnecessarily. A little smile played around on his lips, and there was a glint in his eyes.

'Sorry,' she said again. 'I wasn't looking where I was going.'

Still, he said nothing. He only kept holding her as his smile deepened to reveal a beautiful set of white teeth.

To, what she realised was her annoyance, he slowly started releasing her, so she took a couple of steps back.

'No harm done.' His voice was enticing. 'Are you okay?'

She blinked and nodded awkwardly.

'Ah… I'm fine.'

Snap out of it! He will think you're an idiot.

She cleared her throat and spoke again in a voice that she hoped made her sound more in control of herself, even if she didn't quite feel it on the inside.

'Still in one piece.'

He then glanced down at something on the floor.

'But your phone is not, unfortunately,' he said as he bent down to retrieve it.

'Oh, no,' she said as she saw it. After he handed it to her, she looked at it and started swiping the now cracked screen, hoping that it would still, at least for now, work. Thankfully it did.

Still trying to see what the new limitations of the now broken devices was, Gabriela muttered to herself, 'I can't believe I did that.'

'Don't be too hard on yourself,' he said as he once again bent down to retrieve his gym bag, which had also ended up on the floor. Then he asked curiously, 'Wasn't it you who was hanging around at the door earlier?'

At the mention of that, her head snapped back up to look at him. Once again, embarrassment came over her. 'I didn't mean to spy on you. It's just that I was walking past, I heard that cool music and I was curious about what was going on.'

As excuses went, at least that one was an honest one.

He smiled again, 'I didn't mind at all. I thought that maybe you were a new student.'

How did his voice manage to sound so enticing?

'S...student?' The more she looked at him, the more it was becoming difficult to make simple sentences.

'For the Capoeira class in there,' he said, indicating the room he had just left.

'Capoeira?' She had no idea what the word meant. 'What's that?'

'It's the thing that you saw me doing before. It's

a martial art, but it's also a lot more than that. Are you sure you've never heard of it?'

She shook her head. 'No, never. But it looked very interesting. At first I thought that you were dancing, but after I saw all of the kicks, I wasn't sure anymore.'

At that, he chuckled. 'Well it's kind of a few things mixed into one, a dance, certainly, a martial art, a game, a sport... some people might even call it a little spiritual. Then, there's the music, instruments and singing.'

Gabriela listened to him explain and was enthralled. Not just by how good looking he was, but by this thing called Capoeira that she'd never heard about, but was becoming more and more interested in finding out more about.

'Would you like to come in and see a class sometime? You can also join in too if you want to,' he said.

Did he just invite me in?

She could hardly believe it. This tall, handsome man had just extended an invitation, and she was sorely tempted to accept.

'I... I'm not sure that I can.' She knew that these words were coming out of her mouth, but why she didn't just say, '*Yes!*', she didn't know.

He smiled again as he put his hands into the side pocket of his gym bag and retrieved something. It was a business card.

'Here, take this,' he said as he handed it over to

her. 'We have a class website. Have a look at it and if you're interested, drop by at any of the class times. You can just watch if you like.'

She took the card shyly and looked it over. On one side, there was the same logo that he and those girls had on their clothes. A large yellow circle, with the silhouette of two people in the centre in poses similar to the movements Gabriela had seen him doing when she was looking at him through the open doorway. On the other side, it read, *Jogo Arrepiado Capoeira*, plus a web address and phone number.

Gabriela couldn't believe it. The hot guy had just given her his phone number. Well, not actually *his* phone number, just a number to where there was access to him. This was turning into a far better evening than she thought it would be during the Pilates class. As much as the butterflies had started flapping around in her stomach, she knew there was little to no chance she was going to use the card.

'Thank you,' she said anyway. 'I—'

'Gabriela!' There it was again. Tanya's shrill voice rang out as she rushed over to where Gabriela was standing. 'So sorry it took me so long. I'm going to get changed a.s.a.p.' When Tanya reached Gabriela, she looked up at the man with a look of curiosity. 'Who's your friend?'

Far too quickly, she answered, 'He's not my friend. I mean… we just met. Tanya, this is…a…'

She quickly realised that she did not know her new *friend's* name.

Offering his hand to Tanya, he said, 'I'm Sean.'

A simple name, but it felt like a lot more right now.

Tanya giggled, 'Tanya.'

Then he turned his attention back to her, offering the same hand.

'And you must be Gabriela.'

How the man managed to make her name sound so sensual, she did not know, but she could feel goosebumps rising all over her arms.

'Yes, that's me.'

Their eyes met and held with Gabriela transfixed by the glint in his. Though she tried to, she couldn't quite rip her eyes away from him. There was definitely something about the man that had her hooked already. It took an overly enthusiastic throat clear from Tanya to break the spell. Gabriela blinked twice and was finally able to look away. She looked down at the business card still in her hand.

'Thanks for this.' With another small glance at those breath-taking eyes, she started turning on her heels, intending to follow Tanya back to the dressing room.

Was it hot in here?

'Wait!' he said, stopping her in her tracks.

Half turned, she met his eyes once more.

'Yes?'

'Will you come?' His eyes bore into her, daring her to say '*yes*'.

She smiled and then found what she thought was a compromise. 'I'll think about it.' Gabriela couldn't say for sure, but she could have sworn that she saw something that looked like hope flash in his eyes. After that, she turned and walked away, following Tanya, who had been there watching the encounter. They walked along what suddenly felt like the longest corridor in history. She was desperate to turn around and see if he was still standing there. However, she didn't dare. Somewhere, in a deep part of her, she could sense he was still looking at her leave.

When they reached the changing rooms again, Tanya was the first one to speak.

'Whoa! Who was that hottie?!'

'I don't really know. I glanced into the other studio before the Pilates class and saw him there practicing some kind of dance thing.'

'I doubt that's all. I saw that look he was giving you. It was like he was striping you naked with those dreamy eyes.' Tanya fake-swooned and Gabriela rolled her eyes, attempting to dismiss what Tanya was saying.

'I highly doubt that's true. He was just doing some marketing for his class.'

That had to be it, right?

'Look, he gave me the class *business* card,' Gabriela went on.

'I don't care which card he gave you. That man was interested!' Tanya said, as she jumped into the shower. 'Won't be a minute.'

At that, Gabriela settled on one of the benches to wait for Tanya. With no encouragement from her, her mind started wandering back to relive her short but sweet encounter with Sean.

Sean!

Her mind whispered his name.

That name suits him.

After another twenty or so minutes, Tanya was dressed and ready go. They made their way back out to the main entrance and she prayed they would bump into Sean again. As they walked out into the slightly chilly, pre-spring evening air of Central London, Gabriela searched her memory to remember where she parked her car.

Right.

As they turned, something made her glance in the opposite direction. When she did, she could see a tall figure sauntering off in the distance. She was sure it was Sean. He was wearing casual blue jeans and a dark jacket. He was also carrying the gym bag she had seen him with earlier. With a deep breath and a shake of her head, she followed Tanya and headed to her car.

CHAPTER 2

- meia lua de frente - esquiva -

When Gabriela wasn't spending her time drooling over hot guys in sports centres, she owned and managed an exclusive nightclub in Soho. The day after she met Sean, she found herself sitting in her office trying to get some work done. The only problem was that the image of a certain man's naked, muscly torso kept playing around in her mind. She'd spent maybe, maximum, five minutes in the man's company and already he'd taken up residence in her brain. She picked up the card he gave her that she'd earlier placed on her desk. Passing it from hand to hand, her eyes closed and she recalled, yet again, her night as a peeping Tom. His movements, the sweat that glistened on his skin... it all made him intoxicating!

Shaking her head, she did her best to keep ploughing through the mountain of paperwork strewn across her desk. She had inherited her club, called *La Duquesa*, The Duchess, from her father after he'd retired three years ago. He had owned it for fifteen years before that. It had already been a pretty successful enterprise under her father, Carlos Espinosa. When Gabriela took over, it had gone from strength to strength. *La Duquesa* attracted very high-profile clientele and always maintained the highest possible standards in terms of service, discretion, décor, beverages, and so much more. The club was given that name because it had been her father's nickname for her mother. They had shared a great love, and after she passed, about four or so years ago, Carlos could barely step foot in the club anymore. At the time, Gabriela was the general manager of a chain of restaurants dotted around some high-brow neighbourhoods in the West End of London. After she saw how her father was suffering, she decided to hand in her notice to her boss at the restaurants' HQ and she went into the family business. Her father and mother had built this club together and they'd made it a smashing success. She had dreamed of honouring their legacy while putting her own unique touches onto the place.

Her father immigrated to London from Cuba about thirty-five years ago, originally to attend university. Her mother was a second-generation Afro-Trinidadian, who was also starting at the same university. They had met at a Freshers' party and had been inseparable after that. They'd had a wonderful love story that Gabriela could only ever dream of having one like that herself.

With a quick sip from the glass of ginger ale on her desk, she tried to focus on the tasks at hand. She had to order stock and new equipment, check invoices, delegate tasks for her assistant manager, approve some new designs sent over from her marketing team, reply to correspondences from her social media manager and a whole host of other things she would have to get to as soon as possible. It promised to be a very long day, and as it was a Saturday and their busiest night, the night would be long too. However, she wouldn't have it any other way. She loved her job. She'd been coming here to party ever since she could legally do so, and before then, to help her parents out in the daytime. Her parents would always put her to work. They had wanted to teach her good work ethic. At the time, she just saw it as just more chores. But now that she was running it, she looked back on those early days as a blessing. It had ignited her deep love for this place, and she never took what she now had for granted.

At about four o'clock, she slipped out and headed home to get some rest and freshen up for tonight. She didn't always work on Saturdays nights. Or if she did, she was there for three or four hours when she needed to schmooze with a V.I.P. or whenever matters required her to be there. In this business, it was always about networking and she liked to attract the best guests to her club.

◆ ◆ ◆

It had been months since he'd had a good night out. Of late, he'd spent most of his time building his business. Sean Lancaster owned a string of boutique hotels all across England, Scotland and Wales. The free time he did have was spent attending and teaching classes at *Jogo Arrepiado*, the Capoeira school. He first joined the school as a teenager and had risen up the hierarchy to become an instructor. The blue belt he proudly wore around the waist of his trousers symbolised the level he had risen to.

After teaching another great class earlier, he'd received a call from some of his buddies demanding that he join them for a night on the town. All he had planned was a night in front of the laptop doing some research for locations for his next acquisition. The work he loved so much had kind of put his social life on the back burner. Even though he protested, his friends would not take no for an answer. So, he had gone home to change instead.

'Mate, you've turned into a workaholic. We're going to take you out and find someone of the female persuasion to help you to loosen up,' his best friend Thomas had said down the phone.

So here he was now, at a club he'd never been to before called *La Duquesa*, with music blaring and a very lively crowd. As he cast his eyes around, he could see a sea of scantily clad, beautiful ladies who were revelling in the atmosphere of the club. It was a nice place. It had black walls, but with very tastily placed gold highlights. There were strategically placed black leather booths and a V.I.P. area which he could see roped off upstairs. That was their destination. His friend Thomas, Tom, was a member here and had been raving about the place for a while. After much convincing, Sean had finally relented and turned up.

Tonight, it was him, Tom and four other friends, Mikey, Antonio, Jonathan and Lars. The boys settled into their spot and Tom ordered drinks.

'Two bottles of your best bubbly and keep it flowing!' Tom shouted over the music to their assigned waitress. Tom was an eccentric who liked to party hard. He was the heir to a manufacturing fortune, but he never took any of that for granted. He'd spent more than enough time growing his family's business himself.

Sean took a few sips from his drink when it arrived, continuing to survey his surroundings. The boys were engrossed in telling some kind of story, but his eyes were being drawn to a blonde who was eying him. What she was thinking was very plain to see on her face. The look was very suggestive of her interest in him, but she was not particularly to Sean's taste.

As he continued to take the place in, and from his vantage point obliquely opposite the staircase, he spied a woman from behind walking up. There was something vaguely familiar about the sway of her hips which stirred something deep inside him. She was with another, shorter woman who was dressed semi-formally. They seemed to be surveying their surroundings. As they rounded the metal, industrial-style staircase, Sean had a flash of recognition.

Gabriela!

Ever since he'd met her, he'd spent a tremendous amount of time trying to push her out of his mind. The curve of her hips in form-fitting sportswear, the glow of her skin, her juicy lips and those knockout pair of light brown eyes which he had found extremely difficult to look away from. There was something strangely enticing about her that he hadn't been able to get off his mind. He'd felt so pathetic offering her the Capoeira school's business card, inviting her to come see a class. However, that pretext was all he could think of at that moment in order to try to see her again. He had no idea if she would take him up on his offer, but he felt a need to set his eyes on her once more.

Now, sitting here in this spot, watching as she made her way past the different private sections along the upper platform, greeting different guests as she walked past, Sean felt a familiar stirring below his belt.

As she walked past the section he was in, the shorter woman she was with was holding her attention, and her mane of black curls bounced around her shoulders. Sean's eyes followed her as the black knee-length pencil dress hugged her body. He followed until she seemed to settle at the upstairs bar to the right of where he was sitting. The other woman had moved away and Gabriela was chatting briefly with the barman and other staff that walked by.

She seems to be very well known here. Maybe she parties here a lot, by the number of people she seems to engage in conversation.

Sean wondered if he should go over there and say 'hi'. Well, it would be rude not to, he thought, as he drained the remnants of his Champaign glass. Putting his glass down on the table and shouting out an excuse to the guys, Sean started making his way over to where Gabriela was leaning seductively against the bar.

After walking the club with her assistant manager Chloe, greeting some of her regulars and passing on some instructions to her staff, Gabriela lounged by the V.I.P. bar, surveying *La Duquesa*. The place was as busy as it usually was on a Saturday evening. The drinks were flowing and the dance floor was most definitely not abandoned.

Out of nowhere, she started feeling a tingling sensation along her arms, like her flesh knew something that her eyes hadn't seen yet.

Strange... where did that come from?

Glancing over the rim of the glass of white wine spritzer she had in her hand, Gabriela spotted someone familiar walking over to her.

My God! Where did he come from?

It was Sean, the hot guy from the Sports Centre last night, the one that she had spied on, as he practiced that Brazilian martial art. *Capoeira*, was it? It was like he was walking in slow motion, step after graceful step. As he approached, she felt her breath catch and her throat went dry. She took a gulp of the drink and then put her glass down. The club's multi-coloured spinning lights danced and cast a seductive hue across his handsome face. He stopped about a metre or so in front of her.

'Well, if this isn't a small world,' Sean said.

'It's you.'

'Last I checked.' His little smile, as she said that, made her think that he was enjoying her shock.

'How did you know that I was here?' Gabriela felt that she had just asked a very stupid question, but at that moment, she couldn't think of any sensible ones.

'I didn't.' His smile deepened. 'My best friend, Tom,' he said as he pointed over to his section, 'dragged me out tonight as he didn't appreciate the night of work I already had planned.'

She glanced over to the section that he indicated, and then her eyes were once again drawn back to him. She recognised his friend. He was a member here and she always made a point of familiarizing herself in some way or the other with her members, especially the V.I.P.s.

She managed to smile back at him. 'What a small world.'

'Indeed. I was wondering if I'd ever see you again… and here you are.'

'Here I am.' It was all she could manage as her power of speech was being adversely affected by the tall, handsome man standing in front of her.

He came closer and then propped himself against the bar in the same manner that she had, but only inches away from her. She was sure that he noticed the rapid rise and fall of her chest. From where they stood, they had a full view of the entire club.

'You must come here a lot. I saw you walk past. You seemed to know a lot of the guests here and staff too.'

She giggled and looked over at him. She could see the confusion that passed across his face. 'You could say that.'

'What…'

'I *do* spend a lot of time here. Sometimes it feels like every day.'

'Management must love a regular customer like

you.'

'I'd like to think so.' She turned and faced him then. '*La Duquesa* is mine, Sean. *I'm* management. The owner, actually.'

He faced her now. He seemed genuinely impressed, and for some reason which she could not fathom, Gabriela got pleasure from this. His smile deepened and she could see luscious dimples form on both of his cheeks.

'*Really?* It's a nice place,' he said, casting an eye around the club again. 'And I'm not just saying that,' he added at her raised eyebrow. 'There's a nice vibe here, it's not overcrowded and the DJ is spinning some great tunes. What more could anyone ask for? I like it here.'

'Thanks. I'm glad that you're enjoying yourself. Making sure that my guests are happy is my top priority.'

Was that as flirtatious as she thought it sounded?

Gabriela wasn't sure, but she could feel her cheeks burning up.

He smiled slyly. 'Is that a fact?'

She could see the wheels turning in his head.

'Yes.'

He stepped even closer to where she was. He towered over her. His frame would be intimidating, if his face wasn't so warm.

'Dance with me.'

'W… what?'

How is it possible to stumble over the

pronunciation of a simple word like that?

'I said, "Dance with me". I would like you to dance with me.' He stared her down, daring her to say 'no'.

'I... can't. I'm working.'

'I'm sure the boss won't mind if you take a break.' His smile was full of feigned coyness.

She couldn't help but laugh at his quip. She was sorely tempted to be enfolded in those strong arms and lose herself, but she didn't dare.

'One dance...' His eyes bore into her as he extended a hand to her.

Almost of their volition, her hand started moving up meekly to take his. His palm was cool and sent shivers up Gabriela's arm. He held her hand firmly and started leading her towards the staircase. When they walked past his friends, who were still indulging, she could see their mouths open and looking very impressed with Sean.

Her hand still in his, they descended the stairs and made their way over to the dance floor. There was a hip-hop song playing which she liked, so it was easy to get into the groove. She started slowly swaying to the music. She rotated her hips, waist and shoulders as the up-tempo rhythm required. She loved to dance. That was the easy part. It was just that the hungry look in Sean's eyes as she gyrated was doing a lot of things to her pulse that had nothing to do with the music's bass line.

God, but she was magnificent!

The easy sway of her hips, the inviting curve of her breasts, her closed eyes and the pleased look on her face were making Sean hungry, and not for food. He hadn't been to a club in a little while, but he liked to dance, so keeping up with her rhythmically was not the issue. It was the way her body brushed his as they moved together that was speeding up his pulse rate.

And that's how they continued for about ten minutes. Neither of them seemed to care about the original 'one dance' request. Then, the music changed. Gone was the pumping hip-hop and now it was a much slower-paced soul song by Toni Braxton, *Breath Again*. It meant that he had to take her in his arms. Only fabric separated them. He lifted her arms and placed them around his neck. Then, he wound his own arms around her slender waist. He loved how her body felt against his. They moved to the rhythm, song after song, eyes locked together, hearts pumping.

Then the music changed once again. This time, to salsa. Celia Cruz's, *La Vida Es Un Carnaval*, sent electricity through the entire dance floor and also, it seemed, through Gabriela's spine. She moved like a woman possessed. Her head twisted and turned. Her hips were perfectly in sync with Celia. Salsa was one of his favourite styles of dance, so he spun and dipped her to his heart's content.

Marc Anthony's, *Vivir Mi Vida*, came on next,

and Sean could see the uninhibited pleasure this gave her. A huge smile plastered itself across her face. Her hands were on her hips, rolling them to the rhythm. He liked watching her dance and enjoy herself, and even more so that she'd chosen to dance with him.

Another two or three salsa songs passed, and Gabriela remained captured by the spell of the music. Then, the music died down and the DJ was on the mic saying something which Sean had no interest in listening to. The entirety of his focus was on only one place. It was on the siren standing in front of him, with a glow of sweat on her forehead.

Magnificent!

As the music faded, Gabriela slowly started coming back down to planet Earth.

How long have we been dancing?

She had totally lost track of time. She loved to dance and it was not the first time she made use of the dance floor during a work night. If her friends were in, she gladly joined them occasionally, as was her prerogative. Chloe, her assistant manager, was more than capable of handling anything if she'd decided to take a little dance floor interlude.

This time was different, however. The drop-dead gorgeous man in front of her was looking at her in a way that sent chills up her spine. They were both breathing heavily, certainly as a result of their exploits on the dance floor. But, for her, Sean's laser focus on her and her alone was definitely the reason her pulse was quickening now.

He extended a hand to her, indicating with his head that they leave the dance floor.

She took his hand without hesitation. They moved through the guests and then back up the stairs. As she walked, Gabriela glanced at her watch.

An hour! Madre de Dios!

That's how long had passed since Sean had approached her when she was standing at the bar.

'One dance', indeed.

He led her back over to where his friends still were. When they spotted him, one of them shouted, 'Hey man, we saw you tearing up the dance floor.' He said this as he imitated some salsa moves.

Then another, one whom Gabriela recognised to be Thomas Delaney, the manufacturing heir, spoke. 'I see you've met Ms. Espinosa. How were his moves? Two left feet or what?'

They all burst out laughing at the comment.

Gabriela and Thomas were not friends, but she'd made it her business to introduce herself to and chit-chat with as many of her members as she possibly could. She remembered first acquainting herself with Thomas over a year ago.

'Gabriela, please,' she corrected, preferring the informality of her first name. 'He could hold his own,' she said, looking over at Sean with a huge smile on her face. Then, she realised that he was still holding her hand and she quickly extricated hers from his. A little too quickly, she realised, as she looked over and saw something akin to disappointment cross his eyes.

Before she had too much time to dissect what she saw, she heard a female voice call out her name over the music. It was Chloe and she was with one of *La Duquesa*'s bouncers, Cedric.

'Gabriela, sorry, we need you over at the entrance.'

She turned back over to the guys. 'Sorry, gentleman, duty calls.' She turned to walk off when Sean grasped her hand again. She looked up at him, his eyes intense.

'When am I going to see you again?'

'I...I don't know.' Gabriela's brain struggled to process coherent thoughts again.

'What are you doing tomorrow at two?'

'Nothing in particular,' she said honestly.

'There's a Capoeira class at the same place. If you want, you can drop by,' he said. Then, he quickly added, 'Just to have a look.'

Gabriela thought about it for a few beats.

Why not?

She was so fascinated by the way she'd seen him

move when she'd spied on him. And that enticing music! Independent of what Sean was doing to her pulse rate, Gabriela was interested in learning more about Capoeira.

She gave him a little smile. 'You know what? I think I will.'

He nodded and smiled back.

She dragged her eyes away from his and once again looked at his friends.

'Have a good evening, gents.' Then, she turned and followed Chloe and Cedric towards the entrance. With every step she took, Gabriela could feel Sean's eyes on her. She instinctively knew they were. And as she rounded to the stairway landing, about to descend, she glanced back up towards where she'd left him. Sure enough, he hadn't moved. She could see the desire radiating from him.

She shook her head gently, took a deep cleansing breath, and went into boss-lady mode.

CHAPTER 3

- bênção -

Sean awoke the next morning with a smile on his face. His dreams had been consumed by Gabriela. That figure-hugging dress, her sensual curves and the way she knew how to move those hips.

Intoxicating!

He remembered watching her go back to work, taking command of the situation that had arisen. For the rest of the evening, he caught glimpses of her which had his blood on fire.

What was it about her that made his body react like that?

When it was time to leave the club, he caught her attention once more, not far from the exit.

'See you tomorrow,' he'd said.

And she'd just smiled and nodded in reply.

Now, as he rolled out of bed, dressed only in white boxers, he felt excitement dance around in his tummy. He'd see her later, and he was looking forward to it.

He'd slept in, as he often did on Sundays. After a much-needed cold shower, he sat down in the kitchen for a late breakfast of toast, bacon and eggs and hot coffee. Then, he felt nervousness creep in.

What if she didn't come?

She said she would, but now in the cold light of day, she could change her mind. As was of course, her right.

'Sean, my boy, you're hooked!' He spoke out loud to his empty kitchen.

His two-bedroom Marylebone apartment was very tastefully decorated. Very masculine. He'd moved in there a couple of years ago and had hired an interior decorator to work some magic on the place. It had brown leather sofas, modern art and cream walls. It was most definitely a bachelor pad. Sitting now in his fully equipped kitchen, with every gadget money could buy, he smiled. The very intriguing Gabriela Espinosa was most definitely occupying space in his thoughts.

He got up and started gathering his things for class.

Dressed casually in a white blouse and blue

skinny jeans, Gabriela entered the Sports Centre. She headed over to where she remembered the Capoeira studio was. When she found the door, she hesitated outside as she could see a bevy of men and women entering. They were all dressed in the all-white uniform she remembered, with an assortment of colours of belts around each of their waists. Some were wearing the plain green or yellow. Others had on intertwined yellow and green belts. But only one person wore the blue one. And that person was Sean. She saw him as he rounded the corner, coming from the direction of the changing rooms.

He was walking in slow motion again, all six feet of him. When he saw her, he smiled.

'You made it!' He said in a raised voice, as he still had not reached where she stood. She could tell that he was pleased she was there.

'I guess I have.' It was all she could manage.

When he got close enough, he leaned into her and kissed her on both cheeks. This was a perfectly normal greeting all over Latin America and Spain. She knew this very well, being half Cuban herself. But when *he* did it with her, she endowed it with more significance than she would have at any other time, and with anyone else she'd greeted. As he kissed her right cheek, she took in the scent of his aftershave. It was earthy and suited him perfectly. When he kissed her left cheek, she closed her eyes briefly and breathed him in. He had a heady scent.

'Well, come on in,' he said, ushering her inside. He guided her to the back of the room to a chair and dropped his gym bag next to it.

'You can sit here. I'm glad you're here. I hope you enjoy it. We'll catch up after, okay?' He winked and touched her shoulder reassuringly. Immediately, the spot where his hand had touched so casually tingled with sensation.

'Alright.' It was all that she could manage, but even so, that one word still came out breathy.

Then he turned on his heel and went up to the front of the class and started doing some stretches.

Gabriela surveyed the room. To the front, a mirror covered the entire wall. There were about twenty-five students in the large room. At that moment, they were either stretching or chatting. They all seemed to be in pretty good spirits. Then, another man walked in, probably in his mid-forties. He had a very commanding air about him. He was dressed much the same as the others, except he was wearing a white belt. He walked up to the front left side of the room, Gabriela's left, from her vantage point, and turned on the stereo. Music, very much like what was playing the first time she ever saw Sean, came on with the very same metallic twang.

Then, the new man who entered spoke in a heavy Brazilian accent. '*Instrutor Raposo*, start the class.' By his tone and demeanour, he was definitely the boss.

Then, Sean got up from the floor stretch he'd been doing at that moment and started speaking to the assembled group. 'Okay guys, let's get started.'

Wait! Why did that man call Sean, Instrutor Raposo. So, his name isn't really 'Sean'? What's going on?

Gabriela was truly confused by this unexpected information. She continued watching as *'Sean'* led the group through a series of stretches for about ten minutes. They included arm and wrist stretches; neck, shoulder and back stretches; thigh and feet stretches; hip rotations, jogging around the room, squats, jumps and more.

When that was done, the boss took over, and Sean fell in line with the rest of the class, front and centre. The music itself seemed to cast its own spell over the room.

'Okay guys, follow *Raposo. Ginga!*'

Like something that resembled a military formation, every person started performing a series of movements that looked like they were swaying back and forth and side to side, with their feet connecting with the floor in a triangular pattern, in total precision with each other. She remembered seeing Sean do this too that first time.

'Meia lua de frente. Right side first,' the boss spoke again.

Again, the group followed Sean. This move

looked like a sweeping, high, smooth leg movement which went over as far as it could and then went back to its original placement on the floor. Then they went back into what the boss had called '*ginga*'.

'Left... right... left... right.' He said this for each leg they had to use to perform the kick.

'*Queixada.*'

This kick swung around with a lot more momentum than the first.

'*Meia lua de compasso.*'

This required both hands to touch the floor, with the legs only slightly bent. Then one leg would sweep up off the floor and whip around at high velocity.

'*Armada.*'

This looked like a classic spinning kick without the jump.

'*Esquiva.*'

Everyone seemed to lower their upper body as far as they could above the knees. To Gabriela, it kind of looked like they were hiding or ducking, as one arm always seemed to be shielding their faces.

'*Cocorinha.*'

Now, everyone went down, almost like a squat, but with closed legs. One hand touched the ground to support them and the other was across the face, like they were protecting themselves.

As Gabriela sat and watched, she was so fascinated. They all seemed to move in unison.

She wished that she could get up and join them.

'Okay, two minutes water break,' announced the boss after a while. The group dispersed to various parts of the back of the room where their bags or water bottles were located. Sean walked straight to where she was sitting. A little sheen of sweat covered his forehead.

'Hey, how are you doing? I hope you are not too bored.' There was a note of worry in his voice. He came down on one knee right next to her, as that's where he'd dropped his gym bag. This position brought them almost to eye level. If she reached out, she could touch him.

'Are you kidding me? It's great! I wish I could be up there with you guys,' she said excitedly.

He smiled as he took his water bottle out of his bag and took a drink.

'Thirsty?' He said this while offering some to her.

Not for water.

'No, I'm okay.'

He looked her in the eyes. 'I'm glad you're enjoying yourself.'

Under his gaze at this close proximity, she started feeling butterflies in her stomach, so she found a quick distraction.

'Is... uh... that guy the boss?' she asked, pointing at the man who seemed to hold an air of authority in the room.

Without turning around to see whom she was

indicating, he just seemed to instinctively know.

He said, 'Yes. That's the Master. *Mestre Escorpião*.'

'And is your name *really* Sean?' She asked with a raised eyebrow.

This question seemed to genuinely surprise him, as she could see the look of confusion on his face.

'The *Mestre* called you, *Raposo*.'

Then she saw understanding cross his face, which then transformed into amusement.

'You were sitting here thinking I gave you a fake name?' He chuckled.

'Well... no. Not exactly.' She felt silly, and her cheeks warmed up.

At this, he reached out and put a reassuring hand on her thigh. She knew it was only meant to comfort, but it felt incredibly intimate.

'It's an understandable conclusion. "*Raposo*" is my nickname. Most of us here have one. They are given to us by *Mestre Escorpião*. It's a Capoeira tradition.'

'What does yours mean?' She asked curiously.

'It's Portuguese for "fox".'

She giggled. With a wink and a mock seductive tone, she said, 'Is it because he thinks you're a fox?'

He laughed at her joke. 'No, no. He said that he chose it because he thinks when I play Capoeira, I'm quite sly.'

'Ah, now I understand.'

Does he realise his hand is still on my thigh?

'Do *you* think I'm a fox?' His eyes bore into hers.

Gabriela knew exactly which meaning of 'fox' he was implying, and she also knew that it must just be a joke. But with the combination of those eyes, the hand still on her thigh and his proximity to her, she felt like her entire body was burning up.

'I… I…'

Why can't I speak?

'Ok guys, let's go!'

As if saved by the metaphorical bell, *Mestre Escorpião* called the group back.

Sean patted her thigh and stood up. 'See you in a bit.' And then he headed back up front.

Already her thigh was missing his hand.

For the next twenty minutes or so, the group split into groups of two and worked on various short sequences of movement. They repeated them over and over again in order to get them right. Sean, as well as the *Mestre*, were going from pair to pair, adjusting the stance or arm positions of different people.

Then the group got another short water break, but this time Sean didn't come back to his gym bag. Gabriela wasn't sure if she was happy or unhappy about this fact. He instead, chatted up front with the *Mestre*.

After the break, Sean, the *Mestre* and another student started bringing musical instruments to the front of the class. Two, she recognised as being an African-style drum, and the other was a tambourine. Though the third one looked like a bow to Gabriela, as in, 'arrow and bow', she'd never seen anything like it before.

The *Mestre* spoke again. '*Roda* guys!'

At this, the group all started making one big circle, with the instruments and their players side by side, also a part of the circle. Gabriela wondered what was about to happen.

After Sean placed the large drum into its position around the circle, he left the group and once again started walking toward her.

'Come on up. You said you wanted to join us. Here's your chance.'

She looked at him, suddenly nervous. 'No, no, no! I don't want to make a fool of myself. I wouldn't know what to do.'

He chuckled. 'Don't worry, hun. I'd never do anything to embarrass you. All you have to do is stand with everyone else around the circle and clap to the rhythm.' He took her hand and squeezed it, trying to reassure her. 'And I know you have rhythm!' He said this with a knowing look, obviously referring to last night at the *La Duquesa*.

With that, she felt a little braver, and she went and stood next to him and the rest of the students around the circle.

Then, something amazing started happening. *Mestre Escorpião*, who was in the centre of the musicians, holding the bow-like instrument, started hitting it rhythmically with a narrow stick. The sound that it produced was the metallic sound she remembered hearing in the recorded music. He played by himself for about a minute then the other two musicians joined him with their instruments. After that, *Mestre Escorpião* started singing a haunting tune:

Eu não sou daqui
Eu não tenho amor
Eu sou da Bahia
De São Salvador

After every line of the song, the entire group responded with, '*Marinheiro só*', like a chorus. They were doing 'call and response'. She didn't understand most of what the song meant, but she knew enough to know that they were singing in Portuguese and due to its similarity with Spanish, *marinheiro*, must mean, 'sailor', she thought. The song sounded beautiful. Another thing that was happening along with the singing, was that the members of the school that were not playing instruments, were also clapping to a specific rhythm. Sean indicated to her that she should join in with the clapping. So she did.

Then, Sean left her side and along with another student who was wearing a yellow belt, went and crouched down at the foot of the musicians.

Gabriela wondered what would happen next. She did not have to wait long. She saw Sean look up the *Mestre Escorpião* and then he received a nod.

Then, both he and the other student cartwheeled into the centre of the circle. She watched as they both executed many of the movements they had been practicing earlier and others she'd seen Sean do on that very first day they'd met.

Student after student went into the circle and demonstrated different movements, many of which she hadn't seen before. All of which she was totally transfixed by. It was exhilarating to see how they moved, and the music just created the most breath-taking atmosphere. All along, they clapped and sang. They sang faster songs, and the velocity of the movements changed right along with it. Some of the movements looked so dangerous. She wondered how they didn't collide. Well, most of the time, they didn't. Even then, it was mostly the students who appeared to have a little less experience. Many people had a go at singing lead, playing instruments and doing Capoeira in the centre. But they all sang and sang until they reached a crescendo, and then the music finished.

This is glorious!

Gabriela knew then and there that she wanted to do this, learn this. And be part of this world. The only other time she remembered feeling the kind of thrill she was feeling now was when she was on the dance floor.

The circle disbanded, and then the group members started giving each other hugs.

Beginning to feel a little self-conscious, as she didn't know anyone except Sean, she started backing away, heading back to her chair.

'Gabriela!'

She heard Sean shout her name above the now boisterous school. He indicated with his hand for her to come over to where he was standing with *Mestre Escorpião*. She went over.

'This is my friend Gabriela, whom I was telling you about,' he said to the Capoeira Master.

He told his Mestre about me?

Mestre Escorpião greeted her with a smile and gave her kisses on both cheeks.

'Very nice to meet you,' he said. 'Did you enjoy the class?'

'Oh, definitely! I'd love to come back and try it sometime if that's alright?'

He was tall, though not as tall as Sean. He was also tanned, with short black hair. He was also most definitely from Brazil. That accent was unmistakable.

'We'd love to have you. Anytime,' he said.

The Capoeira master chatted with her amicably for a few minutes as Sean went to get his gym bag. He was very charming.

Then it was time to go. She walked with Sean back out to the corridor.

'Are you hungry?' he asked.

'Starving!' And she was. She'd only had a little piece of toast for a late breakfast.

'Great! How about we go grab something to eat?'

'That sounds good.'

'Do you want to wait for me by the main entrance while I go get changed?'

Then he touched her again on her shoulder and started heading in the direction of the changing rooms. She went to the main entrance as he'd suggested and then sat while she answered some text messages from her friends.

Sean stepped out of the changing room shower and towelled himself off as quickly as he could. He didn't want to keep Gabriela waiting too long. It made him happy that she'd come. Seeing her again, in general, made his stomach flip. From the crown of her curly black hair, to the way those skinny jeans hugged her waist, to the soles of her dainty feet, she was beautiful. When he saw her waiting for him outside the class earlier, he was glad that his anxiety that she might not turn up was not well-founded. He realised that a part of him really needed her to be there today for some reason.

Now, having her wait for him right in this building made him feel happier than he'd felt in a long time. He pulled on his shoes, grabbed his gym bag and headed to where she was waiting for him.

There she is!

She sat crossed-legged, fully absorbed in her mobile phone. That gave him the opportunity to observe her candidly. At that moment, her brow was knitted, as if confused by something she saw on the phone screen. Then her mouth perked up on one side, like she was thinking about what to type. He wanted to learn all of her little quirks.

As if she sensed him coming, she looked up and smiled.

Now that's a smile I could get used to!

'What do you feel like eating?'

'I'm not too fussed. I'm sure I'll be fine with whatever you usually eat,' she said happily.

'You might regret saying that,' he warned playfully. 'Do you like Thai?'

'Love it!'

'How did you get here? Did you drive?'

'No, no. I wasn't up to driving into Central London on a Sunday, so I took the tube.'

'Good. I have my car here so I can take us to the place I was thinking of... if you don't mind,' he hesitated.

Just before they stepped outside, she said, 'Why would I mind?'

'Well, we only met a couple of days ago. I told you before that I would never want to do anything to make you feel uncomfortable.'

She gave him a bright smile. 'Strangely enough, you've made me feel nothing but comfortable. But, thank you for being such a gentleman.'

That elicited a chuckle from him. 'You think I'm a gentleman, huh?'

She was right about him of course. He was raised to always treat women with respect.

He held her gaze for a few more seconds by the door.

'Yes, I do.' Her tone was a little more serious this time. She meant it.

He led her to where he had parked his car around the corner and deposited his bag in the trunk. He drove a recent model, navy-coloured BMW, which he loved. It was spacious, with cream leather seats.

'Nice,' he heard her say, almost under her breath. She didn't voice it louder, so he didn't raise it. He drove her to one of his favourite Thai restaurants. It was only about ten minutes away.

'Good afternoon, Mr. Lancaster,' the host greeted him by name. 'Table for two?'

This seemed to surprise her as her head whipped around to him with a question in her eyes.

'Hello Yok. Yes, for two.'

Then, to Gabriela, as they followed the host to their table, 'I've been here a few times before.'

When they were seated at their table, he could see that she was now biting her bottom lip and there was a shadow in her eyes. Her forehead was also now slightly knitted. He could tell that her demeanour had changed.

He quickly added, 'I've brought *business* associates here before.' An unspoken message passed between them. 'They have a large private dining room upstairs for corporate clients.'

He watched as the shadow slowly disappeared, and her face seemed to relax again like it was before. The last thing he wanted her to think was that he'd brought her to a place he took other women to. And by the way he saw her react, he knew that's exactly what she'd thought.

After they were handed their menus, she said, 'What's good?'

'Everything!' And he wasn't exaggerating. He loved the food here. 'What do you fancy?'

'How about fish?'

'Do you like salmon?'

'Love it!'

'Rice or noodles?'

'Noodles'

He had the perfect suggestion for her. She readily agreed to pan-fried salmon in tamarind sauce with Pad Thai. As it was one of his favourite selections, he had the same. They also decided to share some dumplings.

'I love tamarind. As a kid, whenever my parents took me back to their islands, we always went stalking the food markets looking for the best fruits. Tamarind was one of my favourites.'

Her statement piqued his curiousity. 'And which islands are those?'

'My father is from Cuba. He came here to study over three decades ago and never returned, except for vacations of course.' She said this with a chuckle.

'I bet he must have met your beautiful mother and decided he was never leaving.'

At that, another shadow crossed her face. But this one was different. This one was filled with sadness.

'I'm sorry,' he said. 'If that's not something you want to talk about, I understand.'

She swallowed and then her smile slowly started coming back to her face.

'It's okay… really.' She seemed to want to reassure him. 'You're right, actually. After he met *Mamá*, he refused to move back. How did you know she was beautiful?'

'I assumed that's where you got your looks from.'

Her eyes widened at the meaning in his words, and then he saw the blood rush to her cheeks. He could see that what he'd said pleased her. He quickly realised that that was all he wanted to do… please her. Whether it was with his words or with his body. All of it.

She cleared her throat and then went on. He could see that she did not want to address his compliment, and he let it pass.

'My maternal grandparents came here in the late forties from Trinidad. *Mamá* was born here.

And...' she hesitated. 'And died here too. Four years ago...'

He saw the hand that she had on the table shake. He instinctively took it. Any comfort that he was able to give her, he wanted to.

'I'm sorry to hear about your Mom, Gaby,' he said as he caressed her hand.

She gave him a small smile. 'It's alright. I need to get used to talking about her.'

He nodded. 'Also... do you mind that I called you Gaby?'

'It's okay.' Her smile was a lot brighter this time. 'Actually, a lot of my friends call me Gaby. Don't ever let my father hear you calling me that, though. He hates when people call me that. He's a little sensitive.' She laughed. Clearly a memory was playing through her head.

'Noted!' He realised that he was still holding her hand and let her go.

'He used to say, "That's the name your mother gave you, so that's what people should call you!" Never mind that he almost never called *Mamá* by *her* given name.' She smiled at the memory.

'What did he call her?'

'"*La Duquesa*". He said he called her that because she had very exacting tastes.'

'Ah, that's where your club got its name from.'

She nodded.

After that, their conversation continued to flow easily. They munched on their dumplings and when their main course arrived, she started to eat hers with absolute joy. He loved watching her eat. It was good to see a woman who took pleasure in good food.

She asked him about his background and his life too.

His parents were both lawyers. His mother was in family law, his father in corporate. He had two younger siblings, a twenty-six year old brother and a twenty year old sister. He grew up in west London and now he owned hotels. They both told tales of their wild childhoods and how he'd discovered Capoeira.

'I was going off the rails a bit as a teenager and my father decided that I needed to learn some discipline and have somewhere to place my wild energy. My father's friend suggested Capoeira and then he enrolled me. He would hear no argument. That's how I met, João. By the way, that's *Mestre Escorpião's* birth name. His nickname, *Escorpião*, is Portuguese for scorpion. So, I went, I loved it and I stayed. The rest is history.'

'Wow! I really want to try it out, if it's still okay that I come.'

'Are you kidding? I want you there.' That was one thing he knew for sure.

'Good. And I think I now understand why *Escorpião* nicknamed you "*Raposo*".'

'*Oh*?'

'I saw what you were doing when you were

fighting those yellow belts in the circle. You were tricking, distracting and outsmarting them. They never knew where your kicks were coming from. Very aptly named. You were definitely as sly as a fox.' She giggled then, a sound that Sean was taking so much pleasure in.

He smiled. 'That's the aim of the game. And F.Y.I., the "circle" is called a *roda*. It begins with an 'r', but in many parts of Brazil, their 'r' is pronounced more like an English 'h'. '*Roda*', is Portuguese for "circle". Also, we never say "fight". Remember I told you the night we met that Capoeira is a game too?'

She nodded.

'When we want to face off with someone in the *roda*, we always say, "Let's play".'

He could see that he had her full attention as he explained. This gave him pleasure too.

'When's the next class?' He could see excitement in her eyes.

'There's a beginners class on Tuesday night at six thirty, if that works for you.'

He could see her mentally check her calendar. 'And what time does it finish?'

'Eight.'

She started chewing on her bottom lip.

He couldn't help it. Watching her do that brought about an immediate, primal reaction in him. We wanted to reach across the table and plant kisses all over that lip that she was biting on.

Naturally, he didn't. He didn't want the need he started feeling to scare her off.

'I have some high-brow clients coming to see the club at eight-thirty on Tuesday night. They're looking for a venue for a bachelor party. The club is open on Tuesdays, and they insist that they want to have the meeting with me at a time when the club has people in it. Tuesday is the only night they can make it. So, I'm not sure if I can get back to the club on time if I go to the class on Tuesday.'

Another thing that he realised he knew for sure was that he needed to see her on Tuesday, no matter what.

'What if I promise that after the class, I'll break every speed limit to get you to *La Duquesa* on time to meet your clients? And because I'm such a nice guy, I'll even wait for you until after your meeting and make sure you get something to eat.'

He could see that his proposal had surprised, intrigued and tickled her.

'Can I counter your proposal a little?'

Now he was the one who was intrigued.

'You may.'

'How about after my client meeting, I *make* you dinner?'

He couldn't have been more surprised if he'd tried.

She wants me to come over!

He ached to be alone with her.

'You're inviting me over for dinner?'

'Ye...yeah. You've looked after me so well today that I want to repay the favour.'

Oh...

He could feel his jaw involuntarily tightening a fraction. 'I don't need you to repay me, Gabriela.' He hoped that didn't come out as forced as it sounded to his ear.

'Hey... What's with the harsh "Gabriela"?' She said this while mimicking his tone. This time, she was the one who touched the hand that he'd had on the table. He liked how it felt when she touched him. 'I didn't mean to offend you. I just wanted to show my gratitude. Plus, I love cooking.'

Gratitude...

Not exactly the feeling he wanted to elicit from her right now, but beggars can't be choosers. He decided to accept what she was offering with some gratitude of his own.

'I would love for you to cook for me.'

'Great! It's a date!' Then she blushed again. 'I mean... uh...'

She was still touching his hand and was about to pull away when he grabbed hers. He gently squeezed it to reassure her.

With pure, unabashed desire in his eyes, he said, 'It *is* a date!'

It had been months since Gabriela went on a

real date. Now, she found that excitement was building up inside of her to have her first *official* date with Sean on Tuesday.

They finished their food, Sean paid the bill, and they got up to leave. As they walked past the host, she said to them both, 'Thank you for coming.' And then to him, 'I hope to see you again soon, Mr. Lancaster.'

This time, Gabriela didn't immediately start thinking that this might be the place he brought all the women he must date. When she'd realised that they knew him by name, she was shocked by the wave of jealousy which hit her. She did her best to disguise it, but she was almost sure that he saw it all over her face.

As much as she would have liked to spend the rest of the day getting to know him better, she'd already promised her father that she'd go over to visit him this evening.

They got into his car once more and she gave him the address of her Maida Vale house. Once on her quiet street, she indicated which driveway was hers. He drove up and parked behind her black Mercedes.

'Nice place,' he said as he came around to open her door for her.

Her house was a beautiful, semi-detached, red brick property with a large front garden and driveway.

'Thank you.'

She stepped to the side, and he closed the car door on her side.

Without warning, her heart started racing. Here she was, on her own property, a place that had her imprint all over it, and she was standing here like a shy teenager in from of the cute guy.

'I had a great—'

'Gaby, I—'

They spoke in unison and then both burst out laughing. This helped to ease the tension. He stepped towards her then. She was now between him and his car.

'Oh, Gabriela, Gabriela…' he said, gently shaking his head from side to side.

How was this man managing to make her name sound like the sexiest thing he'd ever said?

'…where have you been all my life?' he continued, stepping even closer. He lifted his hand and slowly caressed her cheek. Of its own volition, her mouth fell open slightly, and she took a much-needed breath in.

It was at that moment that Gabriela knew that he was going to kiss her. She had no objections. He softly held the back of her head, and slowly his own head started to descend. Her eyes closed in anticipation. And then everything stopped. Not the kiss of course, but it was the rest of the world that stopped. She heard nothing else but the sound of his breath and the thud of his heart against her chest. When their lips touched, it was gentle, and soft and Gabriela was entranced. His tongue gently probed her mouth, and he licked every inch of her lips gently. Then he dove in for more. By now, he had her up against the car. The metal should have felt a little cold on her body, but she was burning up. He deepened the kiss even further and her hands went up too, around his neck.

'Gaby...'

She heard him mutter this in between kisses. Her name sounded like dripping honey.

Her hands explored the rippling muscles of his back then she grabbed his arse. It was perfect!

He then started planting kisses down along her neck. She could hear herself pant. She wanted more and yet more of him. Then his tongue come out yet again and licked her neck in slow sensual strokes. Her head fell back in ecstasy.

Because he had her pinned against the car, she could feel every part of him against her body, his rock-hard abs and the obvious signs of his arousal against her stomach. It sent a thrill up her spine to know that she was the one who'd made him so alive.

Then, far too soon, he was pulling away from her. She could tell by the look in his eyes that it was not without a tremendous amount of effort on his part.

'Gabriela, do you see what you've been doing to me?' His voice was ragged, almost pained. 'I've wanted to do that from the first moment I met you.'

His admission exhilarated her.

'You're not the only one.'

He smiled at *her* admission.

'I'd better go.' He stepped a full metre away from her. Her body was none too pleased about this.

'Yes, okay.' It was all that she could manage. She pulled herself away from the car and turned and started walking towards her front door.

'Gaby…' She stopped and turned around.

He continued, 'So… I'll see you in class on Tuesday, right?'

To her ears, he no longer sounded sure about this fact. She wondered why.

She smiled a warm and reassuring smile.

'Of course!' And she meant it.

Once again, she headed for the front door, digging her keys out of her jeans pocket. He waited until her door was open before he got back into his car and started the engine. She stepped inside but didn't close the door until his car was well out of view and had roared down the street directly opposite her house.

With a deep breath and a devilish smile, Gabriela finally closed the door.

CHAPTER 4

- aú -

The next morning, Gabriela woke up feeling excited. She'd had a wonderful time with Sean on their *non*-official date, and she was very much looking forward to seeing and cooking for him on their *official* one.

And that kiss!

A wave of heat rose up her body. She rolled over on her back and giggled like a schoolgirl. When he had her up against his car, she'd felt everything. His rock-hard abs, the firmness of his arse and the unmistakable pressure of his arousal. If he hadn't stopped himself, she wasn't sure that *she* would have. The way she'd been so swept away by ecstasy, that kiss could have grown into a whole lot more.

Sean was definitely a very skilled kisser. For a second, a wave of jealousy hit her. It was irrational and silly, so she pushed it away and then dragged herself out of bed. Grabbing her mobile, she walked into the en-suite. As she activated it, one message got her attention.

> Sean: Good morning, beautiful! I hope you slept well. Thank you for a great time yesterday...

Seeing his message warmed her to her core. Funnily enough, it was the 'dot dot dot' at the end of his message that took her right back to that kiss.

Who knew something as mundane as 'dot dot dot' could turn someone on!

She leaned against her sink and started typing her reply:

> Gabriela: Good morning to you too, Sean. I enjoyed myself...

With that, she giggled again, put the phone down by the sink and then jumped into the shower.

A cold one, I think...

As Sean drove to work the next morning, he found himself whistling. He never whistled! But he was whistling his way through London traffic today.

He was heading over to Knightsbridge to view a property that could potentially be the site of his new boutique hotel. At twenty-one, he'd decided that he wanted to be in the hotel business. Now, at thirty-two, he owned nearly thirty boutique hotels in the U.K. And if the place he was heading to now had enough potential, it would be number thirty. This could be a perfect location to add to his growing portfolio. The Lancaster Elite chain of boutique hotels attracted high-paying guests from all over the world who had very exacting tastes. The adage about the customer always being right was definitely in operation in his hotels. He would check this place out first, and if it met muster, he would bring in his investors. They rarely raised objections in these matters, though. He prided himself on having a keen eye for what his guest would want.

He parked his car at the property, got out and then walked around to the passenger side to make sure he closed in his side mirrors. With a narrow street like this, he couldn't be too careful. As he did so, he caught his own reflection in the car window and he immediately had a flashback of the last time he's stood on this side of the car. It was yesterday and Gabriela was in between him and it. At this most inopportune time, he started feeling incredibly aroused. She seemed to be like some kind of a drug to him. Ever since that moment in the Capoeira studio when he'd realised she was spying on his warm up, he'd been drawn to her. When they'd bumped into each other, literally, later, the feeling had got even more intense.

Get a grip, Lancaster!

'Oh, Gaby, Gaby, Gaby…' He said this softly as he shook his head and walked across the street to the

property.

Gabriela spent the entire day making sure the club was in extra tip-top shape. She had her new clients coming tomorrow night and everything would be perfect. Her marketing team needed her approval for their summer promos and her assistant manager Chloe, had to supervise some maintenance.

In between all of that, she thought about Sean. Every time her routine tasks took her past the dance floor, she saw herself and him there once again. As she inspected the upper level, she looked over to the V.I.P. section where she'd left him with his friends last Saturday, and sure enough, a Sean-sized mirage would appear in her mind.

Now, as she sat alone at home, having a post-dinner glass of red wine and indulging in a documentary on Netflix, she felt anticipation built up inside her stomach. Anticipation that in less than twenty-four hours, she would see Sean again. So, she took a few more sips of her wine.

Tuesday went by painfully slow for Sean. Father Time was clearly messing with him. Every time he checked the clock, it had barely moved. Though, he admittedly checked it quite often. When six o'clock finally arrived, he exited his Mayfair office in anticipation for the evening to come. Gabriela would join him as a student in the Capoeira class tonight. Then, she was making him dinner. He was happy about both of these things.

He arrived at the studio early, and as usual, he started warming up. He usually got there before anyone else due to its proximity to his office. He put on some music and started playing with his imaginary opponent, kind of like shadowboxing.

He couldn't believe it had only been a few days since he'd caught Gabriela looking at him while he was doing the very same thing. The woman had come into his life like a whirlwind and he was having a lot of difficulty not thinking about how it felt to kiss her. And how he wanted to kiss her a lot more… among other things.

Within a short time, the students and *Mestre Escorpião* started filtering in. At six thirty, *Mestre* called the students into position and started the warm up. Sean was in his usual position at the front of the class, but even as he stretched, his forehead creased with nerves. He was nervous because it was now six forty and Gabriela still hadn't arrived. He started to wonder if she had changed her mind. It was her right, obviously, but she had sounded so sure when she said that she wanted to join the Capoeira school. He'd seen her look so impressed by the sport he loved so much. And now it looked like she'd had a change of heart.

His mind started going over all the possibilities. Maybe the strength of his arousal when they'd kissed had scared her off, and she was only being polite... maybe...

Before his mind could conjure up any more fiction, the door at the back of the studio swung open and in walked a flushed Gabriela Espinosa. He hadn't turned around. He saw her through the reflection of the floor-to-ceiling mirror that covered the entire front wall. She was panting hard. She had clearly been running. Sean took a very deep breath in and then out, now feeling a little lighter.

She's here.

Sometimes Gabriela really hated London transport. She was all set to arrive about fifteen minutes early, as she hated being late to anything. She'd made sure that she went online earlier this morning and booked a lesson package on the *Jogo Arrepiado Capoeira* website, packed her gym bag with her workout clothes as well as what she'd later need to go to the meeting with her client and left her office at the club with more than enough time to get to the studio. The public transport gods had other ideas, however. She was *sans* car tonight, as she and Sean had made their plans. Two stops away on the tube from where she needed to get off and the train stopped mid-tunnel. Then, it didn't move. For over twenty minutes, it didn't move. She didn't frequent public transport very often, but tonight of all nights, it had let her down. She didn't want to make a bad first impression. She'd sprinted from the station with the wind at her back. A final burst down the corridor and she pushed the door open. The other students were all stretching as the class had already begun. She dropped her gym bag next to the one she knew to be Sean's. There was only one other guy at the back of the class who, like her, wasn't wearing the white school uniform. They both had on loose-fitting sportswear. Obviously, they were the newbies of the group. She moved to the back row and joined in the stretch.

She scanned the packed room looking for Sean. Sure enough, he was in the same position she'd seen him in at the lesson she'd come to watch. She sought out his eyes in the mirror, and of course, he'd already been looking at her. A silent message passed between them with hers being an apology for being late and his, reassurance that everything was okay.

'Guys, follow me,' *Mestre Escorpião* announced from the front. 'For the new people, please follow *Instrutor Raposo*,' he said, pointing at Sean. Then, the Capoeira master started leading the majority of the group through some moves. Some she recognised from before, and others, she didn't.

Then she saw Sean making his way through the

room to the back where she stood. He came up to her and gave her the customary kisses on two cheeks. She couldn't help but breathe in the woody scent of his aftershave. She smiled at him. He did the same, but added a wink. Then he moved over to the other newbie and introduced himself. She heard him say his name was Matthew. He was tall and slender, with long dark hair in a ponytail. He didn't quite reach Sean's height. He was kind of cute in an obvious kind of way. He wasn't really her type, but she wasn't blind either. She may as well go over and introduce herself as they were both clearly the first-timers.

'Hi. I'm Gabriela.' She said, smiling brightly.

'Matt,' he said, smiling back and shortening his name.

Matt greeted her with two kisses on her cheeks, and then he looked her up and down, lingering a little longer than necessary. She knew that look. Sean was standing right next to her, and she chanced a look up at him. For a fraction of a second, she saw his jaw tighten. It was gone so quickly, she thought she'd imagined it.

Introductions over, Sean was replaced by the authoritative *Instrutor Raposo*. He stepped in front of her and Matt and started demonstrating the fundamental movements of Capoeira.

Ginga, the most fundamental of all. Then, *meia lua de frente, esquiva, cocorinha, negativa, bênção, queixada* and others.

After demonstrating each, he watched both of them closely, adjusting their arm and leg positions accordingly. Though some of the movements were difficult for her to get exactly right, Gabriela found that she was thoroughly enjoying herself. She worked out a lot, and up until her early twenties, she'd trained in contemporary dance as well as in salsa, so she was fairly flexible. She was definitely glad to have had all that dance training as it was coming in quite handy, especially with the height some of these kicks needed to be.

Sean was a great instructor. He showed patience when she and Matt messed up and offered praise when they didn't. Her and Matt even got to play each other. Each of them demonstrated the few moves they had learned so far.

After about forty minutes of training, *Mestre Escorpião* called a water break.

'Well done, guys,' said Sean. 'We're going to play in a moment, so grab some water.'

Matt went towards where his water was, and she and Sean went to where their bags were side by side.

Speaking only loud enough for her to hear, he said, 'I was beginning to worry that you'd changed your mind and weren't coming.'

Her brow furrowed. 'Why would you think that?'

She looked at him and saw that he was being serious.

He didn't answer her. He just shrugged.

'If I say I'm going to do something, I do it,' she said.

Their eyes met and they smiled at each other warmly.

Finally, he spoke again as they grabbed their water. 'So, how did you find it?'

'It was great! Some moves were a little tricky, but with a few more classes, I think I can get better at them.'

Sean smiled at her with a curious look in his eye. Then, just before they were called back for the *roda*, he said, 'I'm glad you're here.'

Mestre Escorpião struck the *berimbau*, the bow-like instrument, and the group settled into the *roda*. He struck it again and again and started singing.

A hora e essa
A hora e essa
Berimbau tocou, na Capoeira
Berimbau tocou, eu vou jogar

Then, everything proceeded much as it did the last time. Two players stepped forward, waited at the foot of the *berimbau* and then started when *Mestre* gave them permission. Everything was a sight to behold.

Kick, escape, trick, outsmart.... Gabriela so admired the skill of these people.

Sean had sent her a few of the song lyrics, so

she happily joined in the call and response… the response part, anyway.

She was so engrossed in what she was watching, the singing and the clapping that she didn't notice that Sean had walked right up to her with an outstretched hand.

Wait… why is he…

Then realisation dawned. He wanted her to enter the *roda* and play with him! She shook her head in silent protest. The last thing she wanted was to embarrass herself. It was her first lesson, after all, and everyone else here seemed so good at the moves, and she still performed some of them a little awkwardly.

'Let's play,' he said.

He stood his ground. His eyes encouraged her. She nodded and then entered.

Okay, here goes nothing…

She started her *ginga* with deep concentration, as she wanted to do her best. Sean came at her with a *meia lua de frente*. His kick came so slowly, much slower than it normally would be, but she knew that he was just being cautious as she was a beginner. She searched her memory for what moves she should make when that kick was coming at her.

Ah, yes, esquiva!

She went low to the right and escaped his kick. Then he came with another and another. She did an *esquiva*, or escape, every time. Then she thought she might as well try a kick of her own. She went in for a *queixada*, the whip kick. He, of course, easily escaped. Then she tried a *bênção.* This kick was more like a high, forward push with the foot, intended to push someone straight back, away from you. This time, instead of *esquiva*, he grabbed hold of her extended foot, which was straight and at about ninety degrees off the floor. He held on to her foot for what felt like forever as she tried to keep her balance. He did it with a sly look on his face.

Ah, there's the fox... He's enjoying this...

To Gabriela, there was something about this situation that was very much like foreplay.

He gently let her go and they played for another minute or so. Then, as was customary, he shook her hand, and she exited. After, he played with Matt too.

For the rest of the *roda*, Gabriela sang and enjoyed the exuberant atmosphere and was sorry when the class eventually ended.

I was definitely meant to find all of this!

Gabriela and Sean went straight for their things and agreed they'd meet at the front as soon as possible. The drive to the club shouldn't be longer than ten minutes or so, but she wanted to have as much leeway as possible, so she hurried to wash off in the shower and get changed into business wear.

He must have done the same because when she

met him out front in under ten minutes, his hair was still wet, except he had on casual, sexy, dark blue jeans, a dark t-shirt and jacket.

The man is magnificent!

With their gym bags safely deposited into the trunk of his car, they sped off into the night.

CHAPTER 5

- chapa - rasteira -

Sean drove in silence for a couple of minutes. He could see that she was breathing heavily. She had obviously rushed in her attempt to get to her meeting on time. For him, it was all he could do not to stare at the rapid rise and fall of her breasts. He shook his head and tried to distract himself from this train of thought, as it would not do either of them any good right now.

'How was the lesson?'

She beamed. 'It was amazing! I can't wait to go again.'

He was very happy to hear this. It felt right that she was there.

She went on. 'Moving between kicks and escapes was a little difficult to get my head around, and to do it all while staying on the rhythm was impossible. I must have looked so awkward, right?'

He didn't need to look at her now to know that she had an uncertain look in her eyes.

'You were perfect!' Sean heard her quick intake of breath and then her slow release. 'It was your first class. You did exactly what you were supposed to do.'

'Thank you!' He could hear the pleasure she felt now in her voice.

When they arrived at the club, he stopped out front so that she could get out.

'I'll wait for you at the upstairs bar, okay?'

She nodded and sprinted inside. He parked his car around that corner and then went inside to wait for her. He ordered himself a scotch neat and settled in for his wait. He was happy to wait. If it meant that he got to spend more time getting to know her, he was happy to.

He sipped on his drink and scrolled through emails on his phone. For a Tuesday night, the place had a decent amount of people. The dance floor was fairly full and most of the V.I.P. sections were occupied.

As he ordered his second drink, he glanced around to see Gabriela in the company of four rather tall men. She was walking around downstairs near the edge of the dance floor, pointing out different things about the club to them. The men were listening but Sean could see that occasionally, one of them kept checking out Gabriela's arse. Inextricably, he felt a surge of anger building up inside. His unfortunate mobile phone had to pay for this, as involuntarily, he'd squeezed it.

Get a grip, Lancaster!

At that moment, Gabriela's gaze focused upwards, as she was pointing out something new to them on the upper tier. It was then that their eyes collided and held for a couple of seconds. She gave him the briefest of smiles and then carried on with her tour.

Sean turned back towards the bar and tried to ignore the way his hormones were raging.

After only waiting for about a half hour, Gabriela came up and tapped him on the shoulder.

'Hey, I'm almost done. My clients are gone but I just have a few bits and pieces to do in my office.' She hesitated for a second before she continued. 'If you want, you can wait for me up there.'

He silently nodded and followed her. She led him to a security-locked door across the upper tier from the bar. She swiped a key card and walked up the internal stairs, which led into a corridor. Her office was the first door.

'You can have a seat if you like,' she said as she led the way inside. It was a large space, very well decorated. It was very warm and feminine, like her.

Would you like a drink, she said as she made her

way over to a minibar, fixing herself a lemonade.

'I'll have the same... driving.'

'I'll be ten minutes, tops.'

'Don't worry. Take your time. I don't mind.' He thought better of telling her that he'd wait for as long as it took if he could just be with her. So, instead, he chose to take a seat on the comfortable sofa on the other side of the room from her desk.

After she handed him his drink, she took hers and sat behind her desk. She wrote some things down and then punched away at her computer. She was in total professional mode, crinkling her nose in obvious annoyance about something that she was looking at. He'd seen so many parts of her so far. There was the dancefloor queen who teased him with those hips; the cool businesswoman, commanding her troops in the club; the Capoeira newbie, so focused on doing her best; and now, the efficient cool-headed woman managing her business and solving problems. Whichever iteration of Gabriela he'd seen, he'd found her sexy as hell!

True to her word, she only took ten minutes, and then she walked over to where he lounged comfortably.

'You ready?' she asked while holding her hand out to him. He took it, rose up to his full height, but he made no attempt to let her hand go afterwards. He respected her work enough to let her finish what she needed to, but only a saint would not now take the opportunity to enjoy her. And Sean knew that he was most definitely not a saint.

'Sean, I—'

He didn't let her finish. From the moment he'd seen her rush into the Capoeira lesson earlier, face flushed; to when he was teaching her the moves; to the moment he held her leg up in the *roda*; in the car and when her bastard client was checking out her arse; every last one, he'd wanted her. He'd wanted her alone, like this, looking at him and him alone the way she was now. Her eyes telling him that she was thinking the same things he was.

None too gently, he brought his lips crashing down on hers, almost overwhelmed by his passion. The only things between them were their clothes. His tongue delved deep into her mouth again and again wanting to discover even more depths of her. From the way she answered each of his kisses with one of her own, to the way her chest moved up and down with the force of her heavy breathing, he knew they were equal in their desires for each other. But because he did not want to rush their night, and with more effort than he'd ever used in his life, he slowly started pulling away from the kiss. Both of their breaths were ragged.

He saw a flash of disappointment flash across her face.

Soon, my beautiful Gabriela, soon...

When their breathing had sufficiently slowed,

and he trusted himself to speak, he asked, 'Ready to go?'

All she did was nod, and this time, *she* followed *him* as he held her hand and guided her out of the office, down the private and public staircases, and then finally through the even busier club. Gabriela waved goodbye at the front door to a woman he knew to be her assistant manager, and then they were gone. They didn't need words. Their bodies seemed to be going on autopilot.

When they were about halfway to her house, he finally asked, 'Did they like what they saw?' His question was not wholly innocent.

'Who?'

He could hear the confusion in her voice.

'Your clients. Did they like what they saw... of the club? Are they going to book it?'

'Uhm, yes. They are. They've officially booked *La Duquesa* for the bachelor party.'

He felt like an arse himself for bringing this up, but he couldn't help himself. 'I saw one of them check out your arse.'

Gabriela's head whipped round and he could see in his peripheral vision that she was staring at him. Then, suddenly, she burst out laughing. It was full-throated. He wasn't sure how he felt about her taking this much pleasure at his expense.

'I own a nightclub, Sean. It goes with the territory.' Her laughter was then replaced by chuckles.

When he didn't speak, she continued, 'Regardless, there's nothing I can do about that.'

'True.' His tone was a little clipped.

Stop acting like a caveman, Sean!

A change of subject was warranted. 'So, what are we having for dinner?'

Thankfully, she moved on. 'I thought maybe sea bass and onion risotto with a side salad. How does that sound?'

'Scrumptious!' Hearing what she was going to make for him relaxed him again. 'I can't wait.'

Home, sweet home!

It had been a long day, and there was a small part of her that was tired. However, the biggest part of her felt excited and happy. Capoeira had been great, and now she got to do something she loved for a man she liked.

Sean brought his car to a halt once again on her driveway and came round to open her door for her. As she took out her keys and started heading for the front door, she realised from the click she heard behind her that he'd just closed his trunk. When she finally pushed the door open, he was right behind her, her gym bag in hand.

'You can drop that anywhere. I'll take care of it later.'

She led him into the living room, turning on the lights as she moved. She loved her home. She enjoyed entertaining friends in it. It was the place she felt the most comfortable and at peace.

'This is me,' she said, swishing her arm around like she was one of the ladies on a gameshow showing off the prizes. Suddenly, she was anxious to know if he liked it. She watched as he slowly took everything in, including the neutral tones of the walls, the artwork, family photos and modern soft white furniture.

'I like it. It suits you. It's warm and welcoming.'

That comment definitely warmed her up. She smiled, blood rushing to her cheeks. She spun around as she began to overheat under his gaze.

'What can I get you to drink?' She asked from behind her living room bar.

'Do you have scotch?'

'Ah, yes. There's some Macallan single malt if you like. I don't drink it, but I keep it for when my father comes over.'

'Your father has good taste.'

'How do you take it?'

'Neat.'

She poured him his drink and also a glass of *Rioja*, her favourite red wine from Spain. She handed him his drink. They clinked glasses, and they gazed at each other over the rims as they took a sip.

'I'd better get cooking. You must be starving!'

He still held her eyes. 'Starving... yes...' Gabriela would bet a substantial amount of money that he wasn't referring to food when he said that. Suddenly a little nervous, she spun around and started heading to the door that led to her kitchen. With every step she took, she knew that he was following right behind her.

She put her wine glass on the counter and started pulling things out of the cupboards and the refrigerator.

'Can I help?' He shrugged out of his jacket and put it on the back of one of the dining chairs. With his arms now exposed, Gabrielle enjoyed the sight of his muscles rippling in his arms.

Focus, Espinosa!

'I'm okay. I won't be long.'

'Sure?'

'Definitely!'

In less than forty minutes, Gabriela had the risotto, sea bass and salad prepared. She'd asked him to set the table and light candles. They ate and chatted freely while sitting across from each other. They talked about everything, it seemed, childhood, career, future ambitions and so much more. It was a long time since she'd had such a comfortable interaction with a man. She'd only known him for a very short time, but if nothing else, she could see them being very good friends.

She got up, ready to clear the table, when he stopped her.

'Wait! Let me. You've prepared me an excellent meal, so at least let me tidy up.'

She nodded and resumed her seat. She watched as he cleared the table and washed and dried the dishes.

How very domestic... I could get used to this...

Before she could stop herself, a giggle escaped.

He turned back to look at her from his position by the cupboards.

'What's so funny?' he asked with an amused look in his eyes.

'Oh, nothing, just reading a text message from my friend Tanya. Girl stuff.'

Thankfully, he seemed to accept that.

'So, uh... should we go through to the living room?' She didn't wait for him to respond. She just got up and headed there. She was feeling nervous all of a sudden.

'Would you like another scotch?' She was already at the living room bar and grabbing the Macallan.

'No.' He was standing right behind her.

Her heart went into overdrive.

'What's wrong, Gaby?' His tone was soft and full of concern.

She tried to relax her face before she turned around to meet his eyes.

'I'm... okay.' Even *she* didn't think she sounded convincing.

He came even closer and brushed his hand along

her cheek, and her quick intake of breath was proof of how much she was affected by it. Then he brushed the other cheek. Another intake. As she looked into his eyes, his desire for her was visible in spades!

'Why are you so jumpy?' Again, softly. 'Would you like me to go?' This time, he was propping up her chin with his index finger so that even if she wanted to, she wouldn't be able to avert her face. She couldn't speak as her throat was getting dry. But she could manage a small shake of her head.

It was at this point that his head started slowly descending to hers. The anticipation was making her legs wobbly. He claimed her lips with gentle probing kisses. Her eyes closed, and she took what he was offering. His lips were soft, and his tongue was delectable. His kiss deepened and became hungrier. Her arms went around his waist as she was desperately in need of support, her wobbly legs no longer willing to support her unaided. He moved his hands through her hair and pulled her yet closer. Then, his tongue started exploring her neck. Her head fell back as his hot tongue licked the soft, warm flesh of her neck.

'*Sean...*' Of its own volition, her mouth gasped out his name. Her insides were in a frenzy.

He paused his ministrations on her neck to look into her eyes again. He frowned.

'Do you want me to stop, Gaby? If you do, you need to tell me now... because the things I want to do to you… I won't be able to stop myself later…' His voice was ragged with need.

She couldn't speak.

'*Gabriela…*' He was pleading with her to answer him.

Instead of speaking, she lifted her trembling hands to the bottom of his t-shirt and slowly started lifting it.

As it came off, it revealed the chiselled frame she remembered as she'd watched him train in Capoeira that first time. This time it was a whole lot better, though. She got to see him up close, to touch and caress him to her heart's content. Then, she trailed her fingers up his abs. She stopped at his now pert nipples and gave one of them a gentle squeeze. He moaned, deep and rich, and she liked it. She lowered her head and gave the same one a playful lick. She heard his sharp intake of breath.

'*Fuck…*' he moaned out.

You like that, I see…

Gabriela felt braver, so she did it again. He sucked in another breath. Then, she covered his entire nipple with her mouth and sucked. When he started to pant hard, she moved to the other one. After all, fair is fair.

Eventually, Sean couldn't take it anymore, so he grabbed her head and pulled it back up to his. His lips came crashing down on hers with the force of a freight train, and she matched his need, kiss for kiss. He unzipped the back of her dress and she gladly stepped out of it. Briefly, he stepped back just so he could take her in.

'Magnificent...'

Then, he gently pushed aside her bra straps and pulled down the lace fabric so that she could fall out. To Gabriela, his eyes looked dark at that moment. He cupped both of her full breasts and went in with his tongue, much in the way that she'd done to him. This drove her wild. She grabbed his head and pulled him even closer, urging him on. He released one breast and then skilfully undid the clasp on the back of her bra with one hand. That hand didn't go back to her breast, however. Instead, it went downwards, seeking out the warm folds at her core. He massaged her over her lacy underwear, and lifted his head, looking deep into her eyes. All she saw there was fire. He put his index and middle finger into his mouth, lubricating them. Then, he moved her underwear to the side and his fingers entered her. Probing, searching, delving... Her eyes flew open with the pleasure of it, gripping his shoulders and sinking her nails into his flesh. She knew that was going to leave a mark on him later, but she didn't care. And, it seemed, neither did he.

He started moving his fingers in and out, at first slowly, but his pace picked up. The pleasure she felt every time he went deeper and deeper inside of her was indescribable. His lips claimed hers again, but not once did the pace of this fingers falter.

Much too soon, she felt a sensation rising up through her which she could not control, nor did she want to. It built and built and built until Gabriela exploded. She screamed out in pleasure as her body convulsed in spasms. She panted and twisted and squirmed, but he did not let go of her, nor did he stop his motion. He drove into her until her screams started to slowly die down.

She held on to him as she could barely stand. When he realised this, he reached down and then lifted her into his arms. She wound her arms around his neck.

'Where's your bedroom?' His voice was husky. 'I'm not finished with you yet?'

She gave him directions, and without much effort, he carried her up the stairs and placed her gently on the bed. Now, he pulled off her panties and kissed her on her upper thigh. His kisses ascended even higher until they reached her centre.

'*Sean...*' Her voice was husky, and she was desperate for him to take her with his mouth, but she didn't want to be selfish. 'What about you?'

He stopped what he was doing and looked up at her. He smiled, knowing exactly what she meant.

'Right now, it's all about you, honey. It gives me pleasure to see you enjoy this. But, thank you,' he said with a wink. Then he went back to work.

Oh so gently, he lifted her folds and teased her with his tongue. Gabriela groaned with excitement. The more he gave, the more she wanted. She gripped the sheets and let out yet another scream of pleasure as he raised one of her legs so that he could have better access. As he had done with his fingers before, he managed to find that spot which ignited her flames again.

How can this possibly be better than last time...

Once again, a lightning bolt of energy shot through her, which caused her to lose any semblance of control.

'*SEAN...*'

As she screamed out his name with her release, Gabriela was unaware of the devilish grin that Sean had on his face as he finally came up for air.

'You're magnificent!' Sean said this as he stood up to his full height. He watched as Gabriela still writhed around on the bed, still in the full throes of her second orgasm. The caveman part of him felt like a conquering hero because he was the one who'd made her feel this way. But the other part was happy for her that she was experiencing such pleasure.

He started undoing his belt and then got rid of what was left of his clothing. He saw her eyes open wide right after he took off his boxers. That gave him pleasure too. He'd already taken a condom out of his wallet before he dropped his jeans. Now, fully sheathed, there was nothing else stopping him from putting his final claim on her body.

When he entered her, she was ready for him. Her body tightly gripped his and it sent chills up his spine. He had no recollection of ever feeling anything quite like what he felt inside Gabriela. He saw her pleasure with every one of his thrusts and it made him feel wild. He was on his knees as he delved deeper into her, with one hand holding onto her breast. She matched her rhythm to his. This gave him pleasure yet again as it seemed that their union was somehow meant to be.

How can this feel so perfect?

Without breaking his rhythm, he lowered himself down to her. He missed having his lips on hers, so his tongue once again sought to possess her mouth. Gabriela wrapped her legs around him and that sent him into overdrive. He gently scooped her up from the bed, once again without missing a beat. He drove into her over and over again, until, like a thunderclap, he had his own release.

'Gaby!'

They say that lightning never strikes twice in one place, but nobody ever said anything like that about thunder. His body convulsed repeatedly, and through the fog in his brain, he heard Gabriela scream out his name as she joined him with yet another orgasm of her own. He gently lowered her back down to the bed, both of their hearts beating hard against their chests. He collapsed on top of her... spent.

CHAPTER 6

- martelo - negativa -

The next morning, Gabriela woke as the daylight was just starting to stream into her bedroom. She winced as she felt sore in more places than one. Then memories of how she had spent her night started rushing back to her.

That may be the best sex I've had in my life!

She smiled and turned over to her side. Sean was nowhere to be seen. A quick glance around the room garnered the same result. He was definitely somewhere in her home as she saw his jeans, no longer on the floor but thrown over the back of the armchair she had in her room. She eased herself out of bed and put on the peach silk robe that she had on the hook behind her door. As she opened the door, she smelled the scent of coffee wafting up from downstairs.

'Hmm...'

When she opened her kitchen door, she saw

something that was a sight to behold. Sean was standing, leaning himself with one hand against her garden door and the other one held what she assumed was the coffee she'd smelled. His gaze was focused outside, so she got the perfect view of his white boxers-clade arse. And that's all that he was wearing.

'Wow!'

What do I have to do to wake up to this view every day?

Though it was only a whisper, he must have heard her because he turned around.

The view just keeps getting better and better!

'Good morning.' A simple enough greeting, but the tone of his voice and the wicked look in his eyes spoke volumes.

'Morning,' Gabriela said with a blush.

'Would you like some coffee?'

She nodded and went and sat down at breakfast bar at the kitchen island. Watching him navigate his way around her kitchen wearing, almost, his birthday suit was very enjoyable for Gabriela.

'Did I wake you?' He asked as he placed a cup of coffee down in front of her.

'No.'

'You looked so peaceful when I woke up, so I decided to be a gentleman and let you sleep instead of waking you with my lips around one of your perfect breasts.'

Gabriela nearly choked on her coffee. Her

temperature immediately started rising.

'Didn't you have enough of me last night?'

'Never,' he said with a wink.

Her mouth started to water.

'Drink your coffee, Gaby. It'll get cold,' he said with a wink.

'It's very difficult to concentrate on drinking when you say things like that to me,' she said giggling.

They spent the next hour or so comfortably enjoying each other's company while eating a breakfast of scrambled eggs and toast. The attraction between them had been almost instantaneous, but more than that, Gabriela could say that she liked him. She liked hearing his opinion on multiple subjects. Plus he was funny, too.

After breakfast, she knew that sooner or later, she'd need to start getting ready for work.

'I've got to get into work early today, so I'm going to go jump in the shower?' They were still in the kitchen, and Sean was doing lovely things to her stomach, as he was still wearing only boxers. Even though they'd made love all night, a part of Gabriela still felt like she was perving on him by the way she couldn't keep her eyes off him, fantasising about rubbing her hands on all of those muscles.

She watched as his eyes lit up and a playful smile appeared on his lips. 'Want some company?'

It wasn't really a question, as he was already getting up from the table and leading her out of the kitchen, up the stairs and into her en-suite.

If they weren't the bosses of their own businesses, they might have gotten into trouble because of how much time they'd spent in there. The shower was hot, but not because of the water. Sean took her lips with a hungry need and she gladly gave in to him. She wasn't sure which of them craved the other more. He lifted her up as the water cascaded all over them from above. She wrapped her legs around him for support. He entered her, and she moaned with pleasure. Their rhythms merged, and Gabriela realised that nothing could be more perfect than how he was making her feel. When they reached their highest height of pleasure, both of their bodies convulsed, and they rode the wave of their release. With another deep, delicious kiss, Sean gently lowered her to her feet. Gabriela took a few seconds to steady her wobbly feet.

'That may be the best shower I've ever had,' she said.

He grinned as he started lathering her and himself with shower gel.

She giggled, 'It's probably best if I apply my own soap, or we may never get out of here.'

He took her meaning and let her look after herself.

When they finally wrapped themselves in some

white towels, Sean exclaimed, 'Shit!'

'What is it?'

'I got so carried away in there… no condom…'

She searched her memory too. 'Oh.'

'I *never* do that!'

She could see that he was annoyed with himself.

'Don't worry,' she said, pointing at her inner, upper left arm. 'I have an implant so you don't have to worry about pregnancy. As for anything else, it was my first time condom free too.' She smiled to herself. 'I kind of liked it,' she said with a wink.

He let out a breath of relief and then laughed at her final comment.

'You did, did you? Noted.'

They both laughed and continued to get themselves ready.

Finally, Sean asked, 'So, am I going to see you tonight?'

'I can't tonight. I have plans with my best friend Tanya. Do you remember the girl I was with the night we met?'

'Ah, yes. She seemed nice. I guess I'm losing you tonight to Tanya then,' he said with mock hurt.

Gabriela knew that he was just joking, but when he said it, she felt an unmistakable fluttering in her stomach, which made her feel rather good. She turned her face away from him at that moment and smiled to herself. She didn't want to give him the impression that she took his comment more seriously than it was meant.

'What about class? Do you think you'll come back soon?'

She mentally searched her schedule. 'Uhm, I'd like to go on Friday night if that's okay.'

He smiled then. 'Of course. I like having you there.'

'I liked being there too. I'm working earlier in the day, but Chloe, my assistant manager, has the night shift.'

'Perfect!'

They finished getting ready, Gabriela in a fitted navy dress and Sean in a spare business suit he always kept in his car in case of emergency. It was charcoal grey and definitely custom-made.

The man is definitely hot in a suit!

Sean got into his car reluctantly after giving her a steaming hot kiss which had her head spinning yet again.

'I'll text you.' And with that, he was gone.

Gabriela had a long day ahead of her, made shorter by her overnight guest. Though her tasks for the day included doing payroll as well as doing staff interviews, both fairly mundane, she felt like she was walking around on cloud nine. And by the fact that members of her staff remarked on her extra good mood, they had noticed it too.

She had a feeling of awareness of Sean everywhere, as she arrived and strode past the dancefloor and also when she went up to her office. She remembered him sitting across her office, waiting patiently for her, and the kiss he gave her after she was done. There was something very intoxicating about Sean Lancaster, and she wasn't sure if she would ever get enough.

It was the early afternoon when her phone buzzed with a message from Sean.

> Sean: Hey beautiful!
> Gabriela: Hi Sean!
> Sean: So, some of us from class are going out on Friday after class. It's kind of a Capoeira family tradition. You up for it?
> Gabriela: Well, I wouldn't want to break tradition, would I? Count me in!
> Sean: Excellent! We usually go to a Brazilian club for food and to dance *forro*.
> Gabriela: What's *forro*?
> Sean: A dance from north-east Brazil where *Mestre Escorpião* is from. I'll teach you.
> Gabriela: Yes, please!
> Sean: Great! Gotta go. See you Friday!
> Gabriela: See you then!

If she wasn't on cloud nine before, by the end of their back and forth by text, she was on the moon.

Later on in the evening, when she was having dinner at a restaurant with her best friend Tanya, the extra pep Gabriela had in her step was plain to see too.

'You're glowing, Gab.' Tanya eyed her suspiciously. 'Either you're pregnant or you've met someone. Or both! Which one is it?'

Gabriela nearly spit out her *Prosecco*.

'Tanya, I'm not pregnant!'

'Ah! So, it's a new man, then! Who is he?'

'Remember that guy Sean from the Sports Centre? The room next to Pilates?'

Tanya's eyes widened when she remembered.

'He was hot!'

Gabriela grinned. 'Yeah, he kinda is. He turned up at *La Duquesa* with his friends the next night. He didn't know it was mine. We had a dance, and then I joined the Capoeira school that he's a member of. I'm really enjoying it!'

With feigned hurt, Tanya said, 'So, you're abandoning me and Pilates for Capoeira and the hot guy next door?'

Gabriela knew better than to take Tanya seriously. 'Sorry, Tan. I don't think Pilates was ever meant for me. The pace is a bit too slow.'

Tanya laughed. 'Yeah, yeah, I know. So… I want to hear all the details.'

Their food arrived, and they got stuck into their pasta salads.

'He's really nice. He owns a bunch of boutique hotels around the country. Lancaster Elite.'

'Yeah, I know them. My sister stayed in one of them when she was up in Scotland last year. She couldn't stop raving about it.'

'Obviously, there's the Capoeira class that he does. He's an instructor. He's been at it since he was a teenager.'

'Ever since I've been going to Pilates, I've seen them walking through the Centre, all dressed in white. At first, I thought it was a cult!' Then Tanya burst out laughing at her own joke.

'Tanya!'

'Just kidding, Gab. I'm glad you're enjoying the class. It's a beautiful sport. Plus, you get a hot boyfriend out of it!'

'He's not my boyfriend!' Gabriela snapped back a little too quickly.

'I think thou doth protest too much.' Tanya winked at Gabriela, who just rolled her eyes and forked more pasta into her mouth. 'So, is he a good kisser?'

Gabriela blushed but did not reply.

'He is!' Tanya was on a roll. 'And... have you done the deed?'

Gabriela kept eating, looking everywhere in the restaurant except at Tanya.

'Dirty girl! Well, I'm glad one of us is getting some!'

Then they both burst out laughing. Gabriela loved Tanya to bits. They'd been fast friends from university and inseparable ever since. No matter what, they'd both always been there for each other.

CHAPTER 7

- ponteira -

The next couple of days went by like a flash. *La Duquesa* kept her fully occupied, and by Friday afternoon, she realised that she had been looking forward to decompressing in Capoeira class, but even more so, to seeing Sean again.

She'd decided to leave her car at home and take taxis today as she'd be out with Sean and the other members of the school. So, gym bag in hand, she walked down the corridor that led to the Capoeira studio and the changing rooms. She'd arrived half an hour early as her body felt so tense that she felt the need for a long stretch. As with the first time she'd been here, as she passed the studio doors, she heard the now very familiar sound of Capoeira music playing. This time, she didn't feel like an imposter as she pushed the door open. Just like that first time, Sean was the only person in the room and once again, *sans* t-shirt. She smiled as she was flooded with memories of the night he'd come over to her house. This time, when he saw her, he stopped the moves he was practicing and came straight over to her. Without a word, he took her in his arms and planted a long, deep kiss on her. All she could do was drop her bag and kiss him right back.

When they finally came up for air, Sean spoke, 'Hey!'

'Hey, yourself!'

'I have something for you.' Sean took her hand and led her over to his gym bag. Next to it was another bag. Gabriela was curious as to what he had for her. He handed the bag over to her, and she pulled out its contents. It was a perfectly folded white t-shirt and white trousers. Emblazoned on them both was the *Jogo Arrepiado Capoeira* logo. Her mouth opened wide in surprise and then formed into delight.

'I hope you don't think I'm being too presumptuous.'

She looked up at him and watched as a multitude of emotions flashed across his face, chief of which was nervousness.

He went on, 'I mean, you're not required to wear the uniform as you've only just started with us. But you seem to be enjoying it, so I thought I'd get you a couple of uniforms. I left the other one in my car. I can give it to you later.'

'I don't think you're being presumptuous at all. It's actually very sweet of you. But how did you know what my size was?' She glanced at the size tags.

He smiled like the cat that got the cream. 'I could guess.'

'Do you make it a habit of guessing woman's sizes?'

On the surface, Gabriela knew her question sounded quite innocent. But there was a part of her that desperately wanted to know the answer.

'Only if they're as cute as you.' He laughed then. 'Go get changed. We can stretch together.'

'Alright.' She did her best to bring nonchalance into her voice and face. She wasn't sure if she had succeeded.

After she got changed, she eyed herself in the changing room mirror.

'Not bad!'

As she was about to walk out of the room, two other girls walked in, looked her up and down, then smiled at her. They then carried on with the conversation they'd been having.

Sean was still shirtless and fantastic when she re-entered the studio. Taking a band from around her wrist, she piled her long curls on top of her head and secured them.

She started her stretches as Sean carried on with his practice. She methodically went through each muscle group. As she rolled back up to standing after doing some floor stretches, she realised that Sean was now standing right in front of her. He came closer and planted a light kiss on her lips. Butterflies started dancing around in her stomach. She placed her hands on his perfect abdominals to steady herself.

'I missed seeing you over the last couple of days...' His voice was husky.

'Did you?' His closeness was making her all tingly inside.

After another light kiss, 'Of course. And you?'

He eased back from her, and she could look straight into his eyes. His desire was clear. Before she could formulate a reply, the door to the studio opened, and the two girls that Gabriela had seen enter the changing rooms before walked in. Only this time, they were fully clad in the white Capoeira school uniform. Finally, it made sense why they had looked at her with a little more than a passing interest in the changing room.

Sean reluctantly took a couple of steps back from her.

'To be continued,' he said, winking at her.

'Sean! *Oí!*' the Asian girl said as they walked over to where Sean and Gabriela were. *'Boa tarde!'*

'Boa tarde, Raposo!' This came from the second girl with long, straight, brown hair. Gabriela detected an Eastern European accent.

Sean greeted them with kisses on both of their

cheeks.

'Oi! Gafanhoto. Gazela.'

'And who's your friend, Sean?' The Asian girl asked, looking at Gabriela curiously.

He met Gabriela's eyes. 'This is Gabriela. Gabriela, this inquisitive one is Jennifer and this is Oksana.'

Gabriela smiled at the girls, and they greeted each other with the customary kisses. 'Nice to meet you.'

'*Você também*,' said Oksana.

Sean's use of the Portuguese words piqued her curiosity. 'Those words are your nicknames, right? It's obvious that *Gazela* means Gazelle, but what about the other word? What does it mean? I'm fascinated about why you get given them.'

Sean smiled and so did Oksana. Jennifer had more of a smirk on her face.

He said, 'Oksana is *Gazela* because of her height and grace. Meanwhile, *Grasshopper* over here was always jumping into other people's business. *Mestre* gave me the honour of nicknaming her, and I think it suits her perfectly, don't you think so, *Gafanhoto*?'

Jennifer playfully punched Sean on his arm. 'One of these days I'm going to get you back for that, Sean.'

'You love it really and you know it!' he said with a chuckle.

'And how long have you two known each other?'

Jennifer eyed Sean with a raised eyebrow.

'I rest my case! Nosy as always, aren't you Jen?' Sean said as he shook his head, going back to doing some stretches.

'You know me Sean, I don't like mysteries.'

Gabriela found that she was enjoying the little exchange. Plus the two girls seemed nice. Jennifer was wearing a green and yellow belt and Oksana, a yellow. She needed to remember to ask Sean what each colour signified.

Soon after, the room started filling up with the other students and *Mestre Escorpião*. As before, the class commenced with a group stretch. Matt, the new guy she had met in the last class was there, plus another guy and girl whom Gabriela assumed were new too, judging by their normal sportswear instead of the school's whites.

Tonight, instead of Sean working with the newbies, he was instructing the main group. The four newcomers, including Gabriela, were being instructed by *Mestre Escorpião*.

Stretches over, *Escorpião* started going over the fundamentals with them. *Ginga, meia lua de frente, esquiva, cocorinha...*

The newbies eventually had to pair off and practice their moves on each other. She was with Matt. Gabriela was having a wonderful time. She and Matt laughed every time they messed up and tried to help each other out the best way they could. The wider group was similarly occupied.

At one point, when she and Matt got into a little laughing fit, she caught Sean's eyes, and he was frowning. Almost immediately, he adjusted his face to a tight smile. She wondered what that was about.

When they broke for some water before the *roda*, Sean came over to her carrying a tambourine.

'Do you want to try out the *pandeiro*?' His smile was a lot more relaxed this time.

'*Pandeiro?*'

'Tambourine,' he answered, translating.

'Ah! Sure.'

Sean demonstrated the simple rhythm required for the *roda*, and she copied it easily. Then, *Mestre Escorpião* signalled that it was time. Sean encouraged her to join the musicians to play the *pandeiro*, with him in the centre on the main instrument, the *berimbau*. He started playing first and sang a hauntingly beautiful song to open the *roda*. His voice really was beautiful. Then, when the student on the drums started playing, he indicated with a nod that she could join in with the *pandeiro*.

It was a whole different experience being one of the musicians tonight. There was an energy that was building in the room, and they were the ones that were driving it. The students in the *roda* playing Capoeira dodged and weaved and tricked their opponents, all with cunning smiles on their faces. At the end of every pairing, they shook the hand of their opponent, touched their chest where their heart is or nodded as a sign of respect to each other.

After a little while, both she and Sean were relieved of playing the *berimbau* and *pandeiro*. She was about to take up a position with the rest of the students around the *roda*, clapping and singing, when Sean stopped her.

'Let's play.'

She accepted his request with an incline of her head. They crouched at the foot of the *berimbau*, waiting for the two students in the *roda* at that moment to finish. When it was their turn, they both did an *aú*, a cartwheel, to enter the *roda*. Gabriela felt a little more confident than in the last class. She executed the kicks that she knew and in turn did an *esquiva*, which was an escape, whenever Sean kicked at her. He did all of these with a cunning grin on his face. Then, she decided to try out a kick that *Mestre Escorpião* had taught them earlier tonight called the *meia lua de compasso*, compass half-moon. This kick involved mimicking a drawing compass shape with your hands wide on the floor, your bottom up, then swinging one leg up and around as if you were drawing a semi-circle with a compass. Then, something happened that she did not expect. Sean easily avoided her kick by going under it. While her kick was still in progress, he slowly hooked one of his own feet around her supporting foot's ankle and pulled, effectively pulling her leg right out from under her. She fell flat on her arse.

Sean grinned and then extended a hand to help her up. She took it and grinned back. She knew that this bump on the behind was part and parcel of the learning process.

As the *roda* wound down, *Mestre Escorpião*, who was now on the *atabaque*, the drum, drastically changed the rhythm. Gabriela recognised the rhythm to be samba.

Someone shouted, '*Samba de roda!*' Then, instead of a Capoeira *roda*, it became a samba circle. The students stopped playing Capoeira but started challenging each other to a samba battle. It reminded Gabriela a little of that famous dance battle in the musical, *West Side Story*. It was so much fun to see. Next thing she knew, the new guy, Matt, grabbed her hand and pulled her into the circle for a dance. He smiled, and she laughed, and they enjoyed themselves. Next, Oksana and another one of the students took a turn in the samba circle. The energy in the room was phenomenal right up to the moment *Mestre Escorpião* took his drumming up to a crescendo, held it there, and then ended the music with one final 'bang'. Everyone was jovial, and hugs went around the room. Even Matt gave her a hug. Caught up in the fun of it all, she happily reciprocated. The only thing that tainted the moment was when her eyes found Sean's when she was still in Matt's embrace. If she didn't know better, she could have sworn his bright blue eyes looked dark. Everyone seemed to be smiling and laughing, except for Sean.

What is up with him?

The impromptu party broke up, and people started to leave. On her way to her bag, one of the girls, whom she had met earlier, started chatting with her.

'Hey, Gabriela, you had some nice moves out there,' said Jennifer happily.

'You weren't so bad yourself.'

'So, are you coming to *Guarana* with us tonight?' Jennifer enquired.

'What's that?

'A Brazilian nightclub. Some of us are going to grab some food and *forro* the night away.'

Gabriela understood now. 'Yeah, Sean invited me. I'm looking forward to it. Though I don't know how to *forro*. Sean said he'd teach me.'

'You'll get it in no time!'

Gabriela and Jennifer chatted away quite happily and then Oksana joined them too.

Then Jennifer asked, 'So, how long have you and Sean been together?'

Gabriela tensed and then tried to keep an easy smile on her face. She and Sean hadn't had that conversation themselves yet and she didn't want to jinx anything by saying too much.

'We're not. I mean, we only met recently.'

A knowing look passed between Jennifer and Oksana. The only thing was, Gabriela was the only one who didn't know what the look meant.

Thankfully, Sean rescued her at that moment.

'Are these two busy bodies bothering you?'

Jennifer rolled her eyes at him. 'We're just keeping your... friend, company, *Raposo*,' she said innocently.

'Sure you were!' Sean smiled sardonically and then laughed.

After that, Gabriela went with Jennifer and Oksana to the changing rooms, where they showered and changed for tonight's festivities.

Before she'd walked out of the studio, though, Sean grabbed her hand, lowered his head and spoke into her ear so that only she could hear.

'I'll meet you out front whenever you're ready.'

Gabriela could smell the scent that was his and his alone. The scent she was now so intimately familiar with. Their eyes met, and a promise passed between them.

Because she didn't trust herself to speak, she only nodded and left with the girls.

CHAPTER 8

- rolê -

Sean stood outside the Sports Centre entrance chatting with five of the other guys from the school, including *Mestre Escorpião*. They were all suitably dressed, semi-formally, for the night ahead. He had elected to wear a navy, long-sleeved shirt, dark trousers and brown leather shoes. It was the unofficial tradition of the *Jogo Arrepiado Capoeira* to go out to dance *forro* on Friday nights. The people who went varied every week and whenever Sean joined them, he always enjoyed himself. Most of the people in the school, he'd known for years and he always felt at ease in their company. They were a little family.

The club they usually went to, *Guarana*, was always buzzing. A bonus was that it also served food, which was perfect because they were always starving after an energised class. The club was also never short of beautiful women who wanted to dance and on occasion, more.

This Friday, Sean realised, felt more special, though. For the hundredth time, it felt, he glanced inside for Gabriela. He'd spent two days without seeing her, and it had been a kind of torture. In this time, he'd been managing an internal audit at his office, meeting with his investors and doing the paperwork to acquire the new Knightsbridge property, and through all of it, the one constant on his mind was Gabriela Espinosa. He'd never met anyone quite like her. She was smart, funny, ambitious and sexy as hell! He couldn't remember the last time a woman had turned him on as much as she had. It was very difficult to keep his body in check whenever he was near her and also, to keep his irritation at bay when he saw the new student Matthew with his hands on her. He'd noted the way Matthew had looked at her that first night. He'd watched as Matthew scanned her up and down with obvious interest. He'd caught himself grinding his teeth. Then, again tonight, as she danced with Matthew in *Samba de Roda* and then he'd hugged her after. He realised that he had no right to feel this annoyed. He had no claim on Gabriela. They'd slept with each other and hung out, but that was it.

Christ, they'd only just met, and he was drawn to her in the most primal way. On top of all of that, she seemed to be enjoying this sport which he loved so much and devoted so much of his life to. She seemed to be fitting right in with some of the senior students too. She fit into his world...

Sean needed to put the matter of Gabriela into perspective. He enjoyed her company, and they obviously had great chemistry. He needed to focus on that and only that.

Not long after, he heard chattering women's voices and looked over to the entrance to see if it was coming from the ladies they were waiting for. It was. They all looked lovely as always, but Sean only had eyes for one of them.

Gabriela!

She was a knockout. She was wearing a burgundy, cocktail-style dress with thin straps and a 'v' neckline that perfectly accentuated her breasts. He held her eyes as she walked out, desire written all over his face.

It was a cool spring evening, so she carried her jacket over one arm and her gym bag in the other. He quickly took the bag from her.

'Wait here,' he told her. 'I'll put our bags in my car. I'll leave it parked here and get it tomorrow.

She nodded. 'Ok,' she said huskily.

Sean left them, went to his car and was back in a flash. The other girls had elected to leave their things in lockers in the Centre or in their respective vehicles. The ten of them piled into a couple of black cabs and arrived at club *Guarana* in under fifteen minutes. It had a great vibe, and the music sounded amazing. They had an area reserved and they quickly ordered some delicious morsels. Sean helped her pick as she hadn't had much experience with Brazilian food. Everything he helped her select tasted amazing. And everyone was nice and welcoming to her, so she felt like part of the group.

When they'd finished their food, the group either paired off and hit the dance floor or were asked to dance by one of the club's other patrons.

'So, are you going to ask me to dance or what?' Gabriela asked. They were the only ones still at the table and Sean had barely taken his eyes off her. Under his gaze, she felt like the most desirable woman in the world.

He inclined his head. 'Yes, I think we should.'

He took her to the dancefloor and gave her a quick demonstration. There were some similarities to salsa, so that made it easier for her. Pretty soon, Sean had swept her around the dance floor, and she was fully enjoying herself. He was an excellent dancer and very good at leading.

After a while, they headed back to the table and before she could take her place next to Sean, Jennifer, Oksana and the other girl with them, Kemi, grabbed her and pulled her back out to join them. The girls had a good laugh. After a song, a couple of guys came over to them and asked Gabriela and Oksana to dance. Gabriela hesitated for a second.

'Go on, Gabriela,' shouted Jennifer encouragingly over the music. Things are relaxed here. Sean won't care. He dances with lots of girls here too.'

Not that she wouldn't have danced with the guy if she really wanted to, Sean or no, as she was a grown woman. Her hesitation was out of a sense to courtesy. And though as yet undefined, there was definitely something between them. Jennifer's words did, however, give the final nudge to not overthink this. She took guy's hand, and they started dancing.

'I'm new to this dance to so go easy on me,' she shouted over the music, but had to get close to his ear to make sure he heard her. He smiled and nodded, and they carried on.

They danced about three songs when Gabriela realised she needed a drink. Dancing *forró* was fun, but the energy of it really took it out of you. She excused herself from her dance partner and headed back to the table. When she got there, Sean was nowhere in sight. Only *Escorpião* and another student, Luís, were there, deep in conversation. She sat down and sipped on her *caipirinha*, an amazing cocktail made with *cachaça*, which is a Brazilian spirit, brown sugar and lime.

She scanned the club, trying to spot Sean. She wondered if he was dancing with someone else, but she quickly realised he wasn't dancing. Then, there was a parting of the crowd and she spotted him from the back over at the bar. And, he wasn't alone. There was a leggy brunette next to him. Her hand caressing his back confirmed that she wasn't just some random club-goer. When she leaned over and started whispering something in his ear, there was no doubt in her mind that he knew her.

Gabriela suddenly started feeling sick to her stomach. She knew she had no right to be reacting this way. Two weeks ago, she didn't even know Sean existed. Sure they'd slept together, and amazing though it was, in the grand scheme of things, it didn't really mean anything. There were no agreements, no declarations, nothing of this nature made between them. He could do as he pleased. They both could.

Suddenly, Jennifer and Oksana dropped down on the chairs next to her, chattering. Gabriela had barely acknowledged them, her eyes still glued to Sean and the woman.

'Where's Sean?' It was Jennifer.

She received no answer from Gabriela, though Jennifer did follow the line of her gaze.

Jennifer went on, poking Oksana with one hand and pointing to where Sean was with the other woman, 'Wait, is that Bruna with Sean?'

'Oh my God,' exclaimed Oksana. 'That conniving little...'

Gabriela's interest swung over to Jennifer and Oksana upon hearing these little titbits.

'Who's Bruna?' she asked.

Jennifer met Gabriela's eyes, 'Well… ah…'

In the very short time that she had known Jennifer, she hadn't come across as a person who was ever lost for words. There was clearly a lot more going on here than Gabriela could ever hope to guess.

'She Sean's girlfriend,' Oksana supplied, her tone almost apologetic.

Gabriela felt like someone had punched her in her stomach, and she got a sudden headache.

'Ex!' Jennifer quickly found her tongue again and added.

But it was already too late. Gabriela had stopped listening to everything after Oksana said the word 'girlfriend'.

She got to her feet shakily, mechanically drained the rest of her *caipirinha* and grabbed her handbag and jacket.

'I'll be back. I need to use the ladies' room.' Gabriela knew that she was lying, but at that moment she really didn't care. All she knew was that she needed to get out of there before she made a complete idiot of herself. She didn't even notice the regretful looks on Jennifer and Oksana's faces before she left the table.

She blindly kept walking. The front door was in the other direction to the bar. She walked as fast as her heels would take her and didn't even feel it when to cool spring air of London hit her face as she stepped onto the street.

The absolute last person Sean wanted to run into tonight was Bruna. But he supposed it made sense to run into a *Brasileira* in a Brazilian club. Hell, it's the same place he had met her in the first place a year and a half ago.

He extricated himself from her as quickly as he could, without being rude and headed back to the table, two drinks in hand, a scotch for himself and another *caipirinha* for Gabriela. When he got closer to the table and saw that she wasn't there, he wondered if she was still dancing with that douche, not that he'd ever met the guy she was dancing with. He just didn't enjoy watching other men touch her. So he'd got up and gone to the bar. He wanted to do anything but watch that guy holding her. And that's where he'd bumped into his ex, Bruna Nazário de Lima.

He put the drinks down and took his seat. A scan of the dance floor told him she was no longer there. And another of their table showed that her little handbag was missing.

She must be in the bathroom, I guess.

Then his eyes fell on Jen and Oksana. There was something akin to guilt written over both of their faces. His brow knitted.

'What happened?' His tone was suspicious.

He'd known these two ladies for a while, Jen for two years and Oksana for nearly a decade. They had joined *Jogo Arrepiado Capoeira* at different times, but they had become fast friends. Even though Oksana had joined with her old university friend Luna, she had made a strong connection with Jennifer too. They were two peas in a pod, and they had a penchant for getting into trouble and doing and saying things they shouldn't. They were like his younger sisters in some ways.

He looked around again. There was still no sign of Gabriela. He looked back at Jen and Oksana and somehow, they managed to look even guiltier.

'Where's Gabriela?' Now he knew for sure something was wrong.

Oksana spoke first. 'Well… she saw you over at the bar with Bruna… and we… mentioned her name… and—'

Jen interrupted, 'Gabriela asked who Bruna was, and this big mouth over here told her she was your girlfriend.'

'You did what?!' Sean shouted.

Jen went on, 'I tried to explain that it was your *ex* girlfriend, but I don't know if she heard that part. She just grabbed her bag and jacket and said she was going to the bathroom.'

Sean jumped into action almost instantaneously. He grabbed his own jacket and headed in the direction of the ladies room. He already had a sinking feeling that he would not find her there.

When he got there, he stopped a woman who was about to go in and asked her to check if there was a Gabriela inside. She came back out within a few seconds and confirmed what, in his gut, he already knew, which was that Gabriela had walked out when she was told that Bruna was his girlfriend.

He had to find her. He went outside and pulled his phone out of his pocket and called her. It rang out and then went to voicemail, her beautiful voice asking him to leave a message. He cut the line and called again. Same thing. So he texted her.

> Sean: Where are you, Gaby?

He waited ten minutes and there was still no reply. He started walking hoping he would spot her somewhere out on the street. But it was a Friday night, and as always the streets of Central London were heaving.

He decided to try again.

> Sean: Please, Gaby, I'm worried. I just want to know that you're alright.

Another ten minutes went by, before his phone buzzed in his hand. It was her texting him back.

> Gabriela: I'm alright, Sean. I wasn't feeling well, so I decided to go home. I'm almost there. It was nice spending time with everyone. Have a good night.

Her words were polite and formal. To his mind, her, 'Have a good night', felt more like, 'Have a good life'. It felt like a break-up.

Sean didn't bother replying. What he needed to say to her could not be said in a text message. He opened a taxi app on his phone and quickly requested one, typing in the drop-off location as the place where his car was still parked. His plan had been to leave it there overnight because he was supposed to be having a few drinks over the legal limit. As it, unfortunately, turned out, he barely had one alcoholic beverage with dinner. So it made sense to go get his car.

Just over a half an hour later, he was pulling into Gabriela's driveway. He sighed and got out of the car. The only light that he could see was the soft glow coming from her bedroom window. He pressed her doorbell and waited.

He waited for a minute or so, and even though her living room light had not come on to signal that she'd come downstairs, he would have bet almost anything that she had indeed come down and was looking at him through the peephole. Not only was he currently illuminated by the security light outside her front door, but also, she most definitely would have heard him enter and park on her driveway.

'Please open up, Gaby. We need to talk.'

When she finally opened the door, what he saw, pained him. She was wearing her silk robe, her face was scrubbed clean of the makeup she had worn earlier, and there was deep sorrow in her eyes. There was nothing that would ever have convinced him that she had not been crying. This pained him even more.

'What do you want, Sean? It's late.' Her voice was hoarse and cracked.

It was only just after midnight. That hardly qualified as 'late' for a Friday night. But he, of course, did not say that. He knew why she had really said it. It was just to get rid of him. Wild horses couldn't drag him away from her right now.

'Can I come in?' He asked softly.

She held his gaze, steel in her eyes now. For a split second, he thought that she would say 'no', and ask him to leave.

What would he do then?

But alas, she didn't. What she did do was step to the side, pulling the door wider so that he could enter. There was absolutely no joy in the action. He entered and was immediately confronted with the scent of her everywhere. He glanced over to her living room bar and got a flashback of making her climax right there. He shook his head, sweeping away the memory. This was definitely not the time for that. How could he not remember, though? Even now, when her face clearly showed nothing but anger and hurt, she still looked so beautiful.

'Can I get you something to drink?' Her voice was emotionless.

'No.' She was doing her best to be polite to him even though she must think he was the scum of the earth.

He took off his jacket, dropped it over the back of an armchair and sat down on the sofa.

'Can we sit and talk?' He said this as he patted the place next to him.

She ignored his gesture and took the armchair opposite him. Something tightened in his chest.

'Gabriela, Bruna is not my girlfriend.'

He saw her quick intake of breath, followed closely by a little light coming back into her eyes. It was gone again before he had a chance to feel hopeful.

'But, Oksana said—'

'I know what Oksana said.' He couldn't let her finish that thought. He didn't want her to be any more upset than she already was. 'Jen told me that she didn't think you heard *her* when she corrected Oksana by saying, "*Ex*".'

At the look of confusion in her eyes, he added, 'Gaby, Bruna is my *ex*, *not* my girlfriend.' He wanted to add that she, Gabriela was the only woman that he was interested in right now, but he didn't. He didn't want to tell her that in the context of this current conversation. He felt that it would be tainted somehow.

'We dated for a year or so, and then we broke up over two months ago. I haven't seen or been in contact with her once since then.'

He watched as a whirlwind of emotions crossed her face before, finally, her body started relaxing a little.

'Then why did Oksana say she was.' Her voice still held a bitter quality.

'Oksana has a dark sense of humour. Every time Bruna's name has come up in conversation over the last two months, Oksana has attached the words "*your girlfriend*" to it. It used to be annoying but then I got used to ignoring it. It seems Oksana got used to it too, and as always, it just came out tonight.'

Gabriela's face was almost completely relaxed again.

'If it makes you feel any better, both Jen and Oksana looked suitable regretfully when they realised what they'd insinuated.' He gave her a weak smile.

Gabriela dropped her face into her hands and shook her head. He immediately got up and went over to her, feeling that now, she may not reject him if he came near her. He pulled her up to her feet and put his arms around her. She followed suit and wrapped her arms around his waist, her face buried in his chest. When he finally pulled back so that he could look her into the eyes, he saw that her eyes were filled with unshed tears. That tightness that he'd felt in his chess before, tightened even more now.

'Oh, baby, please down cry. I couldn't bear it.' He held her close again as he stroked her hair. 'I promise I would never do anything like that to hurt you. I'm not the kind of guy that would sleep around with two women at once.' He wanted her to look into his eye and know for sure that he meant what he was about to say, so he pulled back from her once more.

'There's absolutely only one woman I'm interested in being with, and she's standing right in front of me.'

Finally, he watched as the light came back into her eyes and a small smile formed in the corner of her mouth. The smile didn't completely reach her eyes, though. He could still see the strain there. He lowered his head and gave her a light kiss on the lips. And then another. These kisses weren't intended to ignite passion, but instead to give comfort and convey sincerity.

'Can I make you something thing to drink? Tea, maybe?'

'That would be nice.' She smiled weakly.

'Come on.' He led her over to the sofa and made her sit down, draping a blanket over her. 'I'll be back in a minute.'

She just nodded.

He went into her kitchen and busied himself with the task at hand, all the while ruminating about how spectacularly bad this night had turned out. Gabriela might know the truth now, but she had spent over an hour thinking that he was the worst kind of man. That didn't sit comfortably with him, and he was astute enough to know that it would take more than what he'd told her since he'd got here and a cup of tea for her to be herself again. The cup of chai he made for her would have to be a start. though.

He brought the tea back into the living room and when he saw her, he smiled. In his absence, Gabriela had curled up on the sofa and was now fast asleep with the blanket still covering her. He chuckled and then put the tea down on a coaster on the coffee table.

Gently, he scooped her up in his arms as if she weighed nothing, ascended the stairs and took her to her bedroom. He placed her down on the bed and covered her with the duvet. He turned to leave and then stopped himself.

Would she want him to be there in the bed with her when she woke up?

Uncertainty washed over him, and then he made a decision. He knew he had to risk it. For Gabriela Espinosa, he knew he had to risk it.

CHAPTER 9

- meia lua de compasso -

Gabriela woke with a start. She'd had a bad dream. It was of Sean in *La Duquesa* with his arms around a brunette and his tongue down her throat. She shook her head in an attempt to banish that awful image.

Then her memory fully came back from the night before. Not of *La Duquesa*, as the dream had intimated, but of club *Guarana*. And... what was her name? Bruna. Then her memory shifted to him turning up at her door and then explaining everything. She'd believed him immediately. She could see the sincerity in his eyes. But there was still a part of her that had held onto the twisting feeling she had felt in her stomach when she'd thought he was a lying, disingenuous piece of crap. As much as she'd wanted otherwise, she'd fallen asleep with those kinds of thoughts about him still holding on to a part of her heart. He must have carried her up here because she had no recollection of coming up to bed. It must have been him who'd put her here… and left her alone.

Something twisted in her heart. That was not how she had envisioned last night ending. Not by a longshot.

Glancing over at the digital clock on her bedside table, she saw that it was six o'clock. She was still wearing her silk robe from the night before. She suddenly felt the urge to have a cup of tea, so she headed downstairs. She walked through her living room and spotted something over the back of one of her armchairs. She would know that jacket anywhere. It was Sean's.

Why would he have gone last night and left his jacket behind?

On a hunch, she went to the windows at the front of the house and peeked outside. Her eyes widened. His car was still parked there behind hers.

He didn't leave me alone after all, at least not completely.

The other side of her bed had not been slept in, so he definitely had not slept next to her. A quick search of the kitchen and, once again she came up empty.

Where was he?

Then another thought occurred to her. She padded back up the stairs, and this time, instead of going through to the first bedroom door, which was hers, she continued to her spare room at the end of the hall. When she pushed the door open, she was confronted with a thing of beauty. Sean was lying there, blanket down to his waist, exposing his chest completely. A quick glance around revealed the shirt and trousers he wore last night neatly folded on a chair, his brown leather shoes in the corner. He was snoring softly.

With all thoughts of the tea she'd wanted gone, she disrobed. Wearing only a black bra and underwear, she slipped into the warm bed and snuggled up next to him.

He didn't wake up. He only turned over on his side and out of some kind of natural inclination, wound his arms around her.

As Sean started coming around from his slumber, the scent of juniper started playing around with his senses. It took him a few seconds to remember where he was. He realised that the scent was from Gabriela hair, as she was lying right beside him, fast asleep. She must have woken up and come looking for him. He'd been worried about if she'd want him to stay there at all, but he couldn't bring himself to leave until he knew for sure that she was alright. But he'd wanted to give her space too. Sleeping in her second bedroom was his compromise. Now, waking up and seeing her here with him, he felt relieved.

She was facing him. She looked so peaceful that he almost didn't want to disturb her, but there was another part of him where desire was stirring. He got closer and planted a light kiss on her lips. In her sleep, she wrinkled her nose and let out a soft moan. So, he went in for a second kiss. By the third kiss, she began to come around and smiled groggily. Another few seconds, and he could see the glint of her beautiful brown eyes.

When he saw that she was fully self-aware, he pulled her closer and took her willing lips. He plunged his tongue in her mouth and tasted all that she was offering. His body came alive to her proximity, and he rubbed his hips to her. He wanted her to understand what her presence was doing to him.

They didn't need words. There was a silent understanding that passed between them. They knew that they both needed this. Their night out with friends had gone down the tube and to a certain extent, they knew that they needed to wipe the slate clean and start fresh. What better way to do that than to revel in each other?

He didn't let her lips go as he ran a hand down to her body and nudged her legs apart. He made quick work of freeing her of her lace undies. She was ready for him when he entered her. She let out a soft moan while reaching down to push his fingers even deeper. His lips never left hers as his tongue seemed to harmonise with the motion of his fingers. He finally pulled away from their kiss as he wanted to look into her eyes as she came. He increased the thrust of his fingers exponentially until she stilled, just for a few seconds. Then she let out an almighty scream which pleased him immensely. He watched her ride the wave of her orgasm until, ever so slowly, her panting subsided.

◆◆◆

'You're going to spoil me! Being woken up to that... What more can a girl ask for!'

'The pleasure is all mine. Well... ours.'

She giggled and then took hold of the waist of his boxers. He was wearing one too many items of clothing for her liking. She removed them and got on top of him. She could see that this took him by surprise and she took pleasure in that. She then eased herself down on top of him. She squeezed her eyes shut as she took in as much of him as possible and started moving. Gradually, she increased her pace. She wanted to give him as much enjoyment as he had just given her. She put one hand on his chest and the other behind her on his leg so that she could anchor herself. She rotated her hips and watched as his eyes rolled backward and his chest heave up and down. She then came forward and down. Now, chest to chest, she continued to ride him as he panted with pleasure. Then, suddenly, he grabbed her hips and held them up in place. He then lifted his own hips off the bed, thrusting hard and rapidly. He didn't let up until both of them reached their climax. She collapsed on top of him, utterly depleted.

◆ ◆ ◆

When they finally made it out of bed, it was afternoon. Sean suggested that they spend the day together and Gabriela happily agreed.

'How about a picnic in Regent's Park?' She suggested.

'Sound good to me. But let me swing by my house and grab a change of clothes. I won't be long.'

'While you're gone, I can make us something to eat.'

'Sounds perfect.'

Before long, they got to the park and spread out near the lake. She'd prepared them some chicken baguettes, plus cheese and crackers and some fruit. They happily chatted about their work and Capoeira until Sean's smile sobered.

'Gaby, I really am sorry about the way things turned out last night at the club.'

She wasn't sure if she really wanted to even think about how she'd felt when she thought he already had a girlfriend, but she guessed it would come up sooner or later.

'It's okay, Sean. I know now that it was just a misunderstanding,' she said trying to reassure him. 'Although, at that moment, it *did* make sense, as I'd already seen her caressing your back by the bar.'

This shocked him. 'You saw what?'

She suddenly felt embarrassed. 'She was rubbing herself all over you. Then when Oksana called her your girlfriend...'

'And did that bother you? The, as you put it, the "rubbing"?'

'Kind of, yeah.'

'Good.'

He smiled wickedly and then looked over at the ducks on the lake.

'Is that all you're going to say? "Good"?'

He looked back at her, still smiling. 'I guess now you understand how *I* felt.'

'How you felt about what?' She had no idea what he was talking about.

'Bruna might not have seen me if didn't have any other choice but to leave the table at that moment.'

'Why wouldn't you have had a choice? And what does that have to do with me?'

'*Unfortunately*, I had a perfect view from the table.'

He seemed to be enjoying dragging out whatever it was he was about to say.

'Stop being cryptic, Sean.'

He laughed.

'I had the *perfect* view of you on the dancefloor.'

'*Yeah*, so, I was there.' Slowly, what he was talking about was becoming clear. 'I was dancing… with that guy.' Her eyes widened. 'That bothered you?' She asked, needing to know this more than anything.

'Kind of, yeah,' he said, copying her words.

Hearing him say that put butterflies in her stomach. A smile played on her lips as she, too, now looked over at the ducks in the lake.

'To be clear, you can, of course, dance with whomever you want, I would never ever presume to… it's just that, I wasn't really enjoying the view. Another drink was the only thing that I thought would help at that moment.' Their eyes met and held. 'So I went to the bar.'

Now it was her time to laugh.

'My pain amuses you?' His eyes were alive with humour.

'Don't be dramatic, Sean. It was only a dance.'

'I know.'

'Everyone dances with everyone in a place like that.'

'I know.'

'You shouldn't have let it bother you.'

'Trust me, I know that too,' he said, scooting over closer to her on the blanket, pulling her to him the rest of the way until their faces were inches apart. 'But it bothered me anyway.'

When their lips met, soft, gentle, probing kisses followed. Their heart rates merged, and Sean's tongue savoured her. He had a way of making her weak in all the right places so that nothing else mattered.

The only thing that made them move back from each other, was the public

◆ ◆ ◆

Over the next three weeks or so, no two days in a row went by without Gabriela and Sean seeing each other. She trained at the Capoeira school about three lessons a week, and even *Mestre Escorpião* had remarked as to how well her progress in the sport was going. When she wasn't working the late shift, Sean would pick her up from work and bring her to class or take her out or they'd go back to one or the other's homes.

She wasn't sure if they were maybe going too fast with the amount of time they were spending together. She knew that she certainly had grown so accustomed to having him around. If, for whatever reason, they were not sleeping in the same bed, she would wake up in the morning feeling very lonely and missing him.

The fire that had ignited between them that fateful night when they'd first met had only burned brighter and brighter. Whenever he touched her, even if it was by accident, she'd begin to heat up. She couldn't get enough of him. The intensity of what she was feeling for him threatened to overwhelm her sometimes. Even her father noticed that there was something different about her and said as much on one of their weekly dinners together at their family home.

'*Entonces, háblame de él.*' Carlos Espinoso rarely spoke to Gabriela in any language but Spanish. Tonight was no different.

Gabriela always fluctuated between Spanish and English for her replies.

'Tell you about whom, *Papá*?'

'Whomever it is that has put this happiness into your soul.' Even after all of these decades, Carlos' roots were still strong in his accent.

Gabriela opened her mouth to deny the existence of a 'someone', but she quickly shut it again. It would have been no use. Her father knew her better than anyone else, and he'd be able to tell that she wasn't telling the truth.

'*Está bien.* It's alright. Keep your secrets. Just tell me one thing, *hija*.'

She nodded.

'Does he make you happy?' He asked.

The smile she gave him formed on her lips, but it was also very clear deep within her eyes.

'I think so,' she said. 'But it's early days yet, *Papá*.'

He nodded, seeming to accept that, for now. If

she knew her father, and she did, more questions would be forthcoming in the very near future.

'And does this mystery man have a name?'

Gabriela shook her head from side to side with a smile.

'Sean.'

He hadn't brought it up again that night. They just caught up and chatted about *La Duquesa*. Gabriela had some plans that she'd wanted to run by him.

Another week passed, and tonight, once again, she was training. She had been spending more time with Jennifer and Oksana, the events of a month ago, long forgotten. The three of them chatted happily as they warmed up.

'I can't wait to see the next season of *Bridgerton*. I bet they can't top seasons one or two, especially one.' Oksana was obsessed with the series and could talk for hours about it all by herself.

Gabriela was about to offer a comment when someone walking into the room caught her attention. It was a woman, tall with long, dark brown hair cascading down her back. Gabriela knew that she didn't know her, yet there was still something vaguely familiar about her. The class hadn't actually started yet. She sauntered in, dropped her gym bag and strode confidently to the front of the room. She was dressed in white *abadas*, just like most of the people in the room. Even so, Gabriela knew that she was not a member of *Jogo Arrepiado Capoeira*. This was made clear to her because the belt she wore around her waist was not green, yellow, blue or white, the official belt colours of this school. Instead, the woman's belt was bright red.

She must be visiting from another school.

Of that much, Gabriela was sure. Sean had already taught her about the belts here. The fact that another school's member was visiting was not in itself news to Gabriela. In the five weeks or so since she'd been a part of this school, people had come to visit a few times. She had come to understand that that wasn't something unusual in the Capoeira world. In fact, the higher up the ranks you went, it was actually encouraged.

There was just something about this particular visitor that held Gabriela's interest and she couldn't quite put her finger on it. She kept watching as the woman walked straight up to the front of the room to where *Escorpião* and Sean were standing chatting. It would become obvious that they both knew this woman quite well.

Escorpião greeted her with a smile and two kisses on her cheeks. Then Sean followed suit. However, after Sean greeted her, she didn't step back to allow for personal space. She kept standing right up against him, giving him a hug and caressing his back as she did so. It was a very intimate gesture, born out of knowledge and a connection to the person you were doing it to.

In a flash, Gabriela knew who the woman was. Even though she wasn't close enough to see the woman's face clearly that night at club *Guarana*, there was something in that so familiar, caressing palm on Sean's back that Gabriela would bet a small fortune that this woman was Bruna, Sean's ex-girlfriend.

She's a capoeirista! Why didn't Sean tell me that?

If there was even a smidgen of doubt left as to whom the woman was, two other things happened that confirmed her identity. Sean found Gabriela's eyes from across the room and, the apology that they held was confirmation number one. Number two was the softly uttered curse that came from Jennifer, who was sitting right next to her on the floor.

'*Fuck!* Is that... What the hell is she doing here?'

Gabriela eyes did not waver from Sean's even as he extricated himself from Bruna direct proximity. It was only *Mestre Escorpião* next words which broke the standoff.

'Okay, guys, let's get started. Tonight we're going to be joined by *Instrutora Terremoto*, or Bruna, from *Cordão de Ouro*. Some of you will remember her. She will help us out a little tonight. So, let's go.'

Terremoto... earthquake. I wonder why her Mestre

gave her that nickname...

Despite the way the night was developing, Gabriela managed to keep her focus. She'd fallen in love with Capoeira and was able to immerse herself in it during the first part of the lesson. When it was time, the group assembled itself, ready for the *roda*. This time, however, the musicians sat down on chairs, as opposed to the usual standing. Instead of the one standing drum, the *atabaque*, they used two similar ones, best suited for sitting while playing. There were also two *pandeiros*, or tambourines, this time, and three *berimbaus*, of differing sizes. The entire group was encouraged to sit down on the floor in a large circle too. This was the first time Gabriela had seen the *roda* done this way with her own eyes. The style of Capoeira that *Jogo Arrepiado Capoeira* practiced was called *Regional*. It predominantly required everyone to stand and it usually had a more up-tempo pace of music. But from her own reading and from what Sean had so far taught her, she realised that this time the group was not going to start with *Regional*. They were likely about to do *Angola*, the original Capoeira style. This form is characterised by a slower pace of music, as well as more closed movements, often executed closer to the ground. Gabriela had seen videos of this style, but she was excited to see it now, and live.

Mestre Escorpião started playing his *berimbau* alone and then started singing a *ladainha*, a kind of preparation song, sung at the beginning of *Angola*.

Iê!
Manoel dos Reis Machado
Manoel dos Reis Machado
Foi embora e nos deixou
Deus lhe pôe em bom lugar

From the similarities between Portuguese and Spanish, and also from the fact that she had actively started learning Portuguese herself, she could gather that this *ladainha* was dedicated to a *Mestre* that passed away. It praised him for his skill and what he'd passed down to others. It likened him to a king and said that he would play Capoeira forever in heaven with the other great masters. A lump caught in Gabriela throat as she did her best to loosely translate the song in her head. It was indeed a beautiful song.

As *Escorpião* sang the *ladainha*, Sean and Bruna came to crouch at the foot of the *berimbaus*, the same as she'd seen all the students do in countless classes so far. This time it was different. Bruna's eyes never left Sean's face as they waited for the song to finish. Sean, on the other hand, seemed to be listening intently to the song, not looking at anything in particular. The *ladainha* ended and another song started. Then, *Mestre Escorpião* signalled for Sean and Bruna to enter the *roda* and play.

Her heart tightened in her chest watching this man whom she l—

Gabriela's eyes closed briefly as realisation

hit. Of all the inopportune moments, this was probably one of the worst to realise that you were in love with a man. Now, when they were practicing this beautiful sport with such a rich history, which she had become so attached to. This moment when Bruna, his stunningly beautiful ex-girlfriend was so close, her legs and hands and body glancing off of his as they danced around each other. This was most definitely not the time to realise that you were in love.

Nevertheless, as she sat there on the floor with her knees up, trying to suppress the grip that this irrational jealousy was having on her, even her heart couldn't deny how beautifully Sean played Capoeira with Bruna. They looked perfect together. They looked like they were in a sensual battle of push and pull, attack and parry. They weaved in, out and around each other displaying a level of skill borne out of years of training and dedication. At one point, they both stood on their hands, laser-focused on each other, in a stand-off in which neither was willing to be the first to relent. It was only when their game was finally over that Gabriela realised that she had been holding her breath. She felt the sting of tears behind her eyes, and she willed every ounce of her body to hold on to self-control.

When Sean took his place on the floor around the circle, she could sense that he was trying to make eye contact with her and it took every bit of strength she had not to look at him. She couldn't.

She didn't dare.

After a few more games of *Angola*, it changed back to *Regional* and everyone stood up. The music sped up. Gabriela decided that it was time to put her feelings aside for the moment and to go play. That's why she was there after all.

Without thinking too much about it before she did it, she asked the yellow belt standing next to her to play. The game started off well enough. Gabriela had picked up a lot of moves in the last few weeks and she tried to incorporate them into her game. Then, mid move, the lead singer changed and in a split second, Gabriela realised it was Bruna's voice she was hearing, and it threw her off completely. She lost focus at the same time her opponent came at her with a *meia lua de compasso*, the kick that resembled a drawing compass, where the leg swung up from the floor at a high velocity. Gabriela, in her moment of distraction, moved her face *towards* the kick, instead of escaping *away* from it. The pain she felt in her right cheek was immediate. It was one of the most painful things she'd ever felt.

Immediately, the music cut and a bunch of people ran into the circle to her aid. Her head was foggy and it took a few seconds for her to be able to focus again. When she opened her eyes, she saw that it was Sean in front of her holding her shoulders and others were crowding around too. The last thing she wanted was to be the centre of attention, especially as Bruna had also come over and had placed her hand on Sean's shoulder in a very, to Gabriela's mind, possessive way.

'Are you okay, Gaby?' It was Sean who asked.

She shrugged away from him.

'I'll be fine.' She tried to keep her voice as steady as possible. 'Carry on with the *roda.*' Then, a bit louder so all the group could hear, 'Don't worry. I'm alright, guys. Carry on.'

She walked away from the group heading towards her bag, and the game got underway again. When she got there, she realised that she wasn't alone. Sean was behind her.

'I'll go get you an icepack from the front desk.'

He was clearly concerned, but Gabriela realised that she didn't trust herself to be around him right now.

'No!'

Gabriela wasn't sure if that came out too harshly, so she attempted a smile and tried again.

'Stay here. Please. I'll get it.'

He opened his mouth as if he was about to counter what she said, then he seemed to change tact.

He gently touched her sore cheek with the back of his hand. He looked at her intently, 'Are you sure you're alright, Gabriela?'

'Yes, just stay here, and I'll be back in a bit.'

He nodded, seeming to accept that, then she grabbed her gym bag and headed for the changing room. She knew that there was no way she would go back to play. Her cheek had begun to throb a bit. She thought she might as well change first and then get the icepack on her way out.

She was at the front desk waiting, when Sean came around the corner towards her, still in his whites.

'Is it swollen?' Sean said, coming close.

'No, just a little sore. It was my own fault. Don't worry about it.'

'Of course, I'm worried about it. Why wouldn't I be?'

She shrugged, turning away from him.

'Are you acting like this because Bruna is here?'

'Why would it matter to me if your girlfriend is here?' she asked sarcastically.

'*Ex!*'

She went on as if he'd said nothing. 'Why would it matter that you didn't tell me she was a capoeirista too? And now she's here!' Even to her own ears, she sounded hysterical. 'Why does any of this matter?'

'What are you trying to say, Gabriela?'

'I'm not trying to say anything. In fact, I'd like to say as little as possible right now.'

The receptionist finally came back and handed her the ice pack. She took it and moved away.

'I'm sorry, Gaby, I didn't know she'd be here. She hasn't visited since we broke up.'

'Maybe she has a good reason to visit again.'

She knew the comment sounded a bit childish,

but she couldn't help it. She was still struggling with the realisation that she was in love with Sean and worried that it was too soon.

Sean's gaze narrowed, but he didn't react to what she'd said.

'Listen, I'm going to just head home. I have a long day tomorrow.'

'Let me get changed. I'll take you.'

Sean turned to head for his things.

'No. I'll take a cab.'

'Don't be silly, Gabriela. You came with me, so I'll take you home.'

'You don't need to. I'm sure your... 'friend' wants to catch up.'

Gabriela watched the flash of irritation in his eyes. As if to illustrate her point, she heard a woman's voice call out to Sean. Bruna's rich, accented tone was sultry.

'Sean, a few of us are going to go for a drink and catch up. It's been a while since I saw everyone. You coming?'

He turned to her. 'Maybe another time Bruna.'

'Please, Sean, I need to talk to you about something.'

As much as Gabriela didn't want to be there right now, she couldn't help but observe Bruna's face. It looked strained. There was definitely something on her mind.

'Sean, maybe you should go with her. She clearly needs you,' Gabriela said.

Turning back to Gabriela, Sean said, 'You need me more right now. Clearly you and I need to talk.'

'But—'

'Please don't fight me on this, Gaby. Wait for me, okay?'

She nodded.

Then Sean headed past Bruna, in the direction of the studio.

Before Bruna turned to follow him, she cast Gabriela a look that only another woman could understand. It was a look that said Gabriela was her competition.

Gabriela turned away from her and held the ice pack to her face. She had no interest in being anyone's competition.

Before long, she heard a group of voices coming out towards reception. She glanced over her shoulder and saw that it was made up of most of the Capoeira school, including Sean. Jennifer, Oksana and another woman called Luna, ran over to her.

'Hey girl, how's your face?' Jennifer asked.

'It's alright, just a little sore. It should be back to normal in a couple of days.'

'I can't believe that viper showed up tonight, as if she hasn't done enough damage!' Jennifer sounded furious.

'What damage?' Gabriela asked, intrigued. But before Jennifer could answer, they were interrupted.

'You ready?' It was Sean.

Gabriela nodded, knowing that she wanted to finish that particular conversation with Jennifer. Sean held out a hand to her and she took it. As she turned back to wave goodbye to everyone, she caught sight of Bruna. All Gabriela could see on the other woman's face was undisguised venom.

Perfect! Just, perfect!

She walked hand in hand with Sean, both of them in silence.

On the way to her house, they didn't talk about anything of any consequence. And when they arrived, she poured them some drinks. A glass of *rosé* for her and the single malt for him.

She hadn't asked him much about Bruna before, but tonight she had a burning desire to know everything. So, as they settled in on the sofa, Gabriela didn't censor her questions.

'Why did you and Bruna break up?'

Sean chuckled, 'You don't waste any time, do you?'

'Sometimes direct is best.'

Sean took a sip of his drink before going on.

'She slept with someone else.'

Gabriela spun around to see his face and make sure he wasn't making some kind of joke. He was not.

'But, why? I can't understand why anyone would want to do that to you.'

He smiled wryly, 'I guess I wasn't the one for

her.'

'That's still no excuse.'

They were both silent for a bit before Gabriela continued.

'Where did you meet her? When she visited the school?'

'No, she'd never been there before she met me.'

Gabriela eyed him with mock suspicion. 'Do you bring all the women you're attracted to into the school and encourage them to join in?'

He chuckled again. 'Well, no. That was only you and Bruna. She was already a capoeirista, so it made sense to invite her to visit from her own school. As for you,' he said as he stroked her hands, 'have you forgotten how we meet? You were spying on me through an open doorway and you told me that you liked what you saw. I invited you, *firstly*, because Capoeira has enriched my life and I would always want to do the same for anyone else.'

'And?'

'And what?'

'You said, "*firstly*".'

'You noticed that did you?' He picked up her hand and kissed every finger individually. 'Secondly, because I wanted to see you again.'

Gabriela smiled. 'Wait, you still haven't told me where you met.'

'Believe it or not, we met at club *Guarana*.'

'Really?'

'Yeah. That place is frequented by many

capoeiristas from many different schools. We met, we danced and the rest is history.'

'And now she needs to talk to you. I saw her face. Something's up.'

He seemed to be considering this. 'It doesn't matter. I'm exactly where I want and *need* to be.'

Hearing him say this made her feel relieved and happy. Watching him play Capoeira so beautifully with Bruna, them so in sync, had really done a number on her.

'You guys played a nice game together. You looked good.'

'I know that it bothered you to see us play. But she was a visiting *Instrutor,* it was expected.'

'Please, it's fine, I promise. *Really*. It just took me by surprise to see her there. It will be fine the next time she's there.'

'You think there's going to be a next time?'

'Bruna looked determined. There was something on her mind. And she clearly hates me.'

He turned and looked at her with a knitted brow.

'What makes you think she hates you?'

She smiled. 'Let's just say a woman knows these things.'

'And what reason would she have to hate you? She's never met you.'

'Oh Sean, women don't like when other women encroach on their territory.'

Sean laughed. 'Territory? Bruna has her own

school.'

'Don't be obtuse, Sean. When I say "territory", I mean *you*!' Gabriela shook her head. 'That woman wants you back.'

'I highly doubt that's true. Regardless, Bruna is in my past.'

Am I in your future?

As soon as the thought came to her mind, Gabriela tensed, and Sean was quick to notice this.

'Gabriela.'

'Yes.'

'Is something else the matter?'

'No.' She did her best to keep the panic out of her voice.

'I'm not sure I believe you, but I just want you to know that if there's ever something that's bothering you, you can always come talk to me, alright?'

Gabriela didn't trust her voice, so she just nodded.

They spent the rest of the evening chatting and having a light dinner. Gabriela felt content. There was no doubt in her mind that she was in love with Sean, but she was even surer that it was not the right time to say anything about it.

CHAPTER 10

- queda de rins -

The next morning, a Monday, Sean was sitting in his office trying to get through some paperwork when the intercom buzzed. It was his assistant.

'Sean, there's someone here to see you. She doesn't have an appointment, but she said you'd want to see her.'

Sean had no idea who that could be as he did not expect anyone, so he asked, 'Who is it?'

'It's a Miss Nazário de Lima.'

Sean's hand stilled mid-sentence over the document he was making notes on.

What the hell is Bruna doing here?

He knew that he could not just leave her out there. Gabriela was right. Clearly, there was something that Bruna wanted to say to him, so he might as well get this over with.

'Fine. Let her come through.'

As Bruna entered his office, Sean stood up and went to greet her with a kiss on both cheeks. He had no desire to be anywhere near her, but good manners demanded this of him. One kiss per cheek was customary for Brazilians.

'*Bon dia.*'

'*Bon dia*, Sean.'

Bruna was a financial advisor in the city, so she was dressed in a dark business suit.

'This is a surprise, Bruna,' he said in clipped voice.

'Well, yes,' she said, her tone measured. 'I wanted to talk to you last night, but it seems you had other… *plans*.'

Sean heard the irritation in her voice when she said '*plans*'. Once again, he was realising that Gabriela may have had a point. There did seem to be some sort of animosity here on Bruna's part towards Gabriela. Not that Bruna had any right to feel that way. They had broken up more than three months ago. She screwed someone else, and Jennifer had caught her in the act. When Sean found out about it, he admitted to himself that it hurt his pride more than anything else.

They'd been dating for well over a year. They had many things in common, chief amongst them was Capoeira. She'd grown up in Salvador, Brazil, and as Capoeira was such an intrinsic part of her culture, when they'd met, that was the first thing that bonded them. However, over time, the relationship began to wane. She'd been visiting her family back in Salvador for about a month just before she'd cheated on him. Her trip had given him a great deal of time to think about what he wanted, and he'd already come to the conclusion that the relationship, casual though it might have been, had run its course. Then, one night he'd received a call from Jennifer. She and Bruna worked at the same company. Bruna had only come back from Brazil the day before and Sean hadn't yet had the opportunity to see or speak to her. There was a work post-Christmas party on the same night at her company. Jennifer had walked into what she'd thought was an empty conference room. She'd been looking for a quiet place to take a phone call. What she saw as she entered, was Bruna, post-coital, sitting on the desk and a work colleague she was with, with his trousers and boxers still around his ankles. Jennifer and Sean had been great friends since she had joined the Capoeira school, so she'd called him that same night and told him what she'd seen. Maybe it was some kind of a twisted blessing in disguise. By the next day, their relationship had officially come to an end. Sean hadn't seen her since. At least not until the night at club *Guaraná* when he was with Gabriela.

Now, seeing her again here in his office, a place she'd been to many times before, Sean felt nothing. Yes, she was still beautiful as ever. But there was now only one woman who consumed his thoughts.

'Can I offer you something to drink? Water?'

'Yes, water would be great.'

He looked at her face closely, and there was something he saw there that caused his stomach to knot. Bruna always had a great poker face, but today he saw something close to fear crossed her eyes. He walked to a mini fridge and got her a bottle of water. He indicated to a chair for her to sit and then took his own again behind his desk.

'What can I do for you, Bruna?'

'Ah… well… I… I've not been well recently.'

'I'm sorry to hear that.'

'So I went to the doctor…'

'I hope it wasn't bad news.'

'Well, no, actually.'

Bruna paused for what seemed like forever to Sean. He was eager to have this little catch-up over and done with.

'Bruna, please tell me what you—'

'Sean, I'm pregnant.'

'Okay.' This news didn't particularly faze him. 'Well, I'm very happy for you and… what's-his-name.'

Bruna rolled her eyes. 'This has nothing to do with any "what's-his-name".'

Sean looked at her, confusion written all over his face.

'Sean, it's yours.'

His eyes widened. 'I fail to see how that's possible. We always used protection, and have you forgotten the reason we broke up when we did? Did you take precautions then?'

Bruna had the decency to look ashamed.

'That's beside the point.'

'Bruna, I can't believe you'd stoop this low.'

'Sean, listen. My doctor did the calculations. She said I'm over four months pregnant. If you'll recall, the beginning of the year is when we last slept together. There was no one else but you then.'

The more she continued speaking the more the tightness in his stomach grew. He did his own mental calculations as she spoke, and she was right. She'd spent most of January in Brazil, but they had slept together the night before her flight.

The damn condom must have split. Fuck!

Sean was in shock. His mind immediately went to Gabriela. He wondered what this news would do to them and if it could mean the end of them. Without a doubt, he would do the responsible thing and support his child. But Gabriela was a factor here too. The last thing he ever wanted to do was hurt her. In this relatively short time, she had become important to him. More than that. She was now essential to him. He couldn't just ask her to accept this as a part of their relationship. But he knew he didn't want to lose her.

Bruna must have interpreted what he was

thinking by the look on his face. 'I can see that this news has put a kink in your plans. Well, it's not like I wanted this either. Well, I suppose... what did they say her name was?' Bruna paused. '*Gaby!* Well, she won't be pleased with this little inconvenience. I guess you're going to have to say goodbye to that one.' Bruna's voice reeked of pure hatred, and it was directed at Gabriela. Sean didn't remember Bruna ever being this nasty.

'Her name is Gabriela! And she's absolutely none of your business.' Sean's voice wanted to make it clear that he'd have no one speak ill of Gabriela.

'Well, I'm the one who's carrying your kid. She *is* my business.'

'Listen, Bruna, I have a lot of work to get through. Let me call you tomorrow, and we can talk all of this through, alright?'

'Now you're trying to get rid of me?'

'No, Bruna. I'm not trying to get rid of you. This is a lot to process. I just need a little time. Could you give me that?'

The anger on Bruna's face dissipated a little.

'Fine!'

She got up and headed to the door with Sean trailing her.

Bruna then turned and looked at him, her hands going up to touch his chest.'

'You know, I still care about you, Sean. I know I screwed up big time before. What I did was stupid and a giant mistake. I would never do that to you again. I promise. If you would give me another chance, I know that we could make this work and raise our baby together.'

He was still in shock about this pregnancy, and it was going to take some time wrap his head around the fact that, like it or not, he was going to be a father in a matter of months. He didn't want to hurt Bruna, but he knew he needed to be honest her too.

'Bruna, I can't yet say what's going to happen with you, me and this baby, but please, I need you to understand something. Gabriela and I are serious. As long as she'll have me, I'm going to be with my girlfriend.'

Bruna's face hardened again. 'Don't fool yourself Sean. You're little girlfriend is going to go running in the opposite direction when she finds out that you now come with baggage.'

Bruna then turned and walked out of his office. Sean closed the door and then leaned up against it for support. This was the very first time he'd referred to Gabriela as his girlfriend. It felt right to say it. But he couldn't deny that what Bruna had said about Gabriela running away from him when she found out, had made an impression on him. That could be exactly what happened. And there would be nothing he'd be able to do to stop her. This was *his* mess. Not that he really considered his child a 'mess', but the situation was definitely messy.

Sean went back to his desk and tried to get back to work. But it was no use. His mind was in total turmoil. He replayed everything Bruna had told him, and he started to panic at the thought of what Gaby might do. Doing any actual work today was turning out to be a lost cause.

Gabriela planned to be at class on Tuesday evening. But the night before, she received a call from Sean, and he said that something had come up and that he couldn't go. He'd insisted that she go, regardless. Something sounded wrong with him, but he'd insisted that she had nothing to worry about. He added that there was something he needed to talk to her about. Gabriela wasn't sure if it was something good or bad, but the cryptic nature of his words had her feeling a little anxious. She consoled herself with the knowledge that he'd talk to her about it as soon as he was ready.

So, she made the decision to go without him. It's not as if they were joined at the hip.

The class was amazing, as always. She learned a few more moves, played the *atabaque* and played in the *roda* with Oksana and Jennifer. The only negative to the lesson was that, once again, Bruna had shown up. Gabriela felt thankful that at least

Sean wasn't there tonight, and Gabriela didn't have to watch Bruna's overly familiar hands touching any part of his body. Bruna was a pro, so no more nasty looks passed between them during the lesson. However, as Gabriela headed to her car after class, she heard someone call out her name. It was Bruna, of course.

'Gabriela. Can I talk to you?'

The absolute last thing Gabriela wanted to do was to speak to this woman. She was only a few feet from her car. She didn't stop or turn around until she had the key in the lock.

'How can I help you, Bruna.'

When Gabriela met her eyes, Bruna's were pure steal.

'Listen, you don't know me, and I don't know you. What I know is that my baby will need its father, and you being around will get in the way of that.'

'Excuse me?'

What the hell is this woman talking about?

'Don't play dumb. I know Sean has told you by now. He won't have time to play boyfriend-girlfriend with you. He'll be too busy being a father to our son our daughter. So back off!'

As Bruna spoke, she began to gently rub her stomach, the tell-tale gesture of pregnancy.

Suddenly, Gabriela felt sick to her stomach. But she didn't dare betray what she was feeling to this woman.

'The only person that can make me back off is Sean.' Gabriela said this with more conviction than she felt. She knew there was only one place she could get answers to what was going on. And it was not from this clearly manipulative woman. 'Good night.'

Gabriela got into her car and drove away. She knew there was only one place she needed to go right now. And that was to see Sean. The man she loved owed her an explanation for what that woman had just intimated. Was it really true that she was pregnant with Sean's baby? Was she really malicious enough to lie to Gabriela about being pregnant, especially as it was so easily disproven? More importantly, why did she have to find out about it from Bruna? Sean had given her a spare key to his apartment as she'd been spending so much time there. If he wasn't at home, then this would be the perfect evening to use it for the first time.

Sean had spent the last two days with his mind in a state of turmoil. Bruna showing up and dropping her bombshell had thrown him completely. When she'd visited the school again for the first time in months, this was the last thing he'd have expected to hear. He knew he wanted kids one day, maybe, but he at least thought he'd be a bit more settled before that happened. After work, he just wanted to be alone, so he'd found himself in Hyde Park, walking by the Serpentine lake, trying to figure out his next steps. He had to tell Gabriela, and soon. He cared about her and wanted to be with her, but he knew that maybe this would be too much for her to handle. This is why he couldn't go to class tonight. That is where Gaby would be, and he didn't know if he was ready to see her yet, knowing what he knew and then inevitably, when they'd be alone after class... He just needed a little more time.

After his walk, he went to a quiet pub in Central London. He was would up and needed to take the edge off. It wasn't until ten-thirty when he entered his apartment complex in Marylebone. He was rounding the car park heading to his private parking space when he realised that someone was in his spot. When he drove closer, he knew instantly whom the car belonged to. It was Gaby's Mercedes. Immediately, his heart started to thud faster inside his chest.

Sean drove past his private parking space and headed for the visitors' parking area. He knew he wouldn't be able to be around her all night without telling her. He realised that this was going to be a long night.

Gabriela had been waiting for Sean for a couple

of hours, but she had busied herself with making and eating a sandwich and also catching up on some work on her laptop. She was sitting on Sean's brown leather sofa, punching away at the keyboard, when she heard keys in the door. She looked up at him as he entered, a tight smile on her face. His own face looked grim, and his eyes held sadness.

'Hi.'

'Hi Gaby.'

'Is it okay that I came over? I know we didn't have plans to see each other tonight, but I needed to speak to you, so I took the chance and came.'

'I'm glad you're here.'

She put down her laptop on his coffee table and stood. He pulled her to him and held on to her tightly.

'Are you sure? You don't look like you're in the mood to see anyone right now.'

He pulled back and smiled, though it didn't quite reach his eyes.

'I'll always be happy to see you.'

She nodded and stepped away from him.

'How was class?' He asked. She could hear the strain in his voice.

'Good. No injuries.' She smiled now too, but she knew her smile didn't reach her eyes either. There was a gigantic elephant in the room.

Here goes...

'Bruna was there again.' She eyed him, hoping

to find no reaction from him at all, which would be a sign that Bruna was lying through her teeth. Instead, upon the mention of Bruna's name, Sean's eyes flew up, and she saw something akin to fear, cross his face. She'd never seen him react to anything with fear before.

Bruna wasn't lying. She is pregnant… The man I love is going to be a father… and it isn't mine…

'Why didn't you tell me, Sean? Why did I have to find out like that?'

His eyes closed, and he shook his head as if to clear it of an unpleasant memory.

He opened them again. 'Let's sit.' He indicated the sofa where she had just been sitting.

'I'm very sorry you found out like that. If I'd known she would go to the school tonight, I would have made sure to tell you myself, before she pulled something like this. As she finally told me what she was trying to tell me a few days ago, I didn't think she had any reason to go back there. I'm sorry, Gaby.'

She nodded.

'She showed up at my office yesterday. Then she told me she was over four months pregnant and it was mine.'

When he said the word 'pregnant', the sickness she'd felt in her stomach earlier came back.

When Gabriela spoke again, she barely recognised her own voice.

'I thought you said the first time you didn't wear

protection was with me.'

'It was. But I guess the last time Bruna and I were together fit into that .1 percentage fail rate.'

Neither of them said anything for what felt like forever to Gabriela.

'You're going to be a father Sean.' Her voice was almost a whisper.

He shook his head. 'I know.'

'You didn't want kids?'

'I thought maybe I would have one, one day. But not like this. Not by accident. Not with someone I wasn't in a relationship with. But I guess this is how it was meant to be.'

'I guess you must have a lot to think about.'

'I'm sorry, Gabriela.'

'Why?'

'Because I know you didn't sign up for this.'

'The most important thing here is that your child will be born in... five months.'

Five months...

Gabriela looked away from him, instead focusing her attention on her hands. They were shaking.

She continued, 'I'm not important compared to that.'

'The baby is the most important, you're right. And I'm going to do my best to be a good, responsible father, but please don't ever say you're not important. No matter the context, you're important to me.'

Gabriela glanced up at him. She knew that he was being sincere.

'Sean.'

'Yes.'

She knew she needed to ask her next question. Though it was purely out of a sense of self-preservation, she felt she had no other choice.

'I know this might sound a little selfish, and maybe it is... Plus, I haven't yet had a chance to think about what I want to do.' She knew she was rambling, but she couldn't help it. 'But... does this mean that you have made plans to go back to Bruna? Because if you have, please tell me now. It would be a lot better for all concerned if I know now. Then we can all get on with ours li—'

'Is that what you want, Gaby... to get on with your life?' It sounded like these words were being ripped out of him.

They looked deep into each other's eyes, neither of them saying a word. Gabriela could feel tears threatening at the back of her eyes, but this was neither the time nor place to become an emotional wreck. Deep down inside, she knew those tears would have to be shed, but that time wasn't now.

'I don't know, Sean. I'm still in shock. I'm sure you are too. There's a lot for you, and *us*, to think about.'

'There is.' He took her still shaking hands. 'To answer your question, Gabriela, I have no intention of going back to Bruna, not in that way.

She will be the mother of my child, and as such, she will be in my life. I will look after them both and be there for my son or daughter, but Bruna and I are over as a couple.'

'I don't think she knows that, Sean. She wants you back. She stopped me outside the Sports Centre after class tonight as I was headed for my car. She said she was pregnant with your baby, and then she told me to back off.'

His jaw hardened. 'She did what? I'll talk to her and make sure she doesn't bother you again.'

'Please don't. She's only doing what she feels is right for her child. I get it.'

'Gaby, it's killing me that you're being so nice about all of this. You must be so angry.'

She smiled and shrugged. 'I feel many things right now, Sean, but not anger.'

'What *do* you feel?'

'Well, I'm not very good at sharing.'

'Sharing?' He looked puzzled

'*You*.'

'Oh. You won't need to share me with Bruna. If I'm honest, the writing was on the wall for us well before she cheated on me.'

'But I *would* have to share you with Bruna, wouldn't I? You'll be a package deal, forever.'

'I know. And it wouldn't be right for me to ask you to just accept any of this. I just know that I want you in my life.'

She nodded. 'Um, I'm going to go. I need time

to clear my head.' She got up, grabbing her laptop from the coffee table. She glanced at him and saw the anguished look in his eyes. As much as a part of her wanted to comfort him, the other part of her didn't have the capacity. She suddenly felt tired and overwhelmed by this news. She hoped that getting some distance from the situation might give her a bit more clarity.

'I understand,' his voice was grim. 'Would you mind if I walked you to your car?'

'You don't have to.' She didn't want him to feel obligated.

'Gabriela, I want to.'

She nodded silently.

After they stepped outside into the hall, he took her hand. His palm was warm, and he gently squeezed hers. They walked down the hall, neither of them speaking, the air thick with tension. When they got to her car, he put her things on the back seat.

Then he turned back to her and pulled her to his body. He cupped the back of her head and kissed her. It was, at first, a slow, deep, searching kiss. She gladly let him kiss her, and she kissed him back. It then became hungrier. Despite the anguish of the situation they'd been discussing, when their bodies connected like this, it was easy to forget all the bad and give in to the fire that overtook their defences.

She groaned as his tongue probed her mouth.

She wound her arms around his back, caressed his muscles and pulled him even closer. She'd never been drawn to any man quite like she was to Sean. He was like a magnet which she was powerless to resist. Did she even want to? She clung to him, desperate for the connection, desperate to forget all that she'd learned. She loved him, and needed him, and her body wanted him so much, that she thought she'd burst if she couldn't have him. Her heart pounded loudly in her chest. His matched hers. All sensible thought vanished when he kissed her like this.

'Sean...' His name left her lips in a groan as he moved to worship her neck with his lips and tongue. Gabriela realised that right now, nothing else mattered except what they both clearly needed.

'Sean... take me back upstairs.'

He'd heard her through the panting and ragged breaths. He raised his head from her neck and searched her eyes.

'Are you sure, baby?'

She was the first to break away. She grabbed her briefcase and handbag from the car again and locked the door. She wanted to go up now before reality dawned again and she changed her mind.

'Yes, Sean, I'm sure.'

He snapped into action, taking her things from her, grabbing her hand and turning back towards the building. His pace was quicker than hers, and she did her best to keep up. It was the longest elevator ride in the world, ever.

As soon as his apartment door shut, he dropped her things on the floor and grabbed her instead. He started undressing her right there in the hall. She knew he couldn't wait, and neither could she. They left a trail of all of their clothes from his apartment door to his bedroom floor. He pushed her down to the bed and got on top of her. There was no need for any foreplay. They needed this right now. He was erect, and she was aching.

He entered her swiftly. Her body welcomed him. He drove into her with reckless abandon, driving deeper and deeper, rotating his hips, making this all the more pleasurable for her. Her body was in a frenzy, as a whirlwind of sensation washed over her. With every thrust, she groaned and panted and begged him for more. Their eyes met as she writhed. She saw his need written all over his face as he gyrated and drove her wild.

As she hit her climax, she was overcome by the emotional struggle of the evening. Her body released all the pent-up anguish, but her eyes also released some hot tears at the same time. She was powerless to control it as it flowed slowly. Before she realised what she was doing, she admitted something to him which, if it had been any other time, she might not have.

'I love you, Sean.'

It was a whisper. She wasn't even sure he'd

heard her. She felt like her confession hung in the air, suspended around them as he kept on thrusting inside of her. He opened his mouth to say something, but before he could, his own body went into spasms as he gave in to his own release. She could see by the way his eyes tightened, and his torso convulsed that his climax was intense. He dropped forward, supporting himself upright on straight arms as he rode the tide. He let out a final ragged breath before he collapsed next to her.

He kissed her on her cheek and encircled her in his arms, pulling her close. Their breaths matched as they both slipped into slumber.

CHAPTER 11

- macaco -

Gabriela awoke with a start. The room was dark, but she remembered exactly where she was. Equally, the memory of Bruna's revelation came back and once again, she felt a sickness in her stomach.

Sean was still asleep. It must still be late or early, as the case may be. Using the moonlight coming through the windows as an aid, she extricated herself from his arms and found her way over to the bedroom door. Before she walked out, she turned and cast one more look at him, making out his shape in the dim light. Her heart was in pain. She knew that she couldn't be here when he woke up. She didn't regret their love making, but a part of her wished she'd got into her car earlier, after all, and left. She needed to clear her head as now it felt more muddled than ever.

She walked through his apartment, picking up items of her clothing that'd been abandoned. She dressed as quickly as she could and put on her shoes. She retrieved her phone from her bag so that she could check the time. It was just after four in the morning. She went into his living room, searched in the drawer of his sideboard for a pen and paper. Once she located them, she sat down and started writing.

> Sean,
> I'm so sorry that I'm leaving in the middle of the night. I woke up and I just needed to go. Please forgive me for that. There's so much that's going through my mind right now that I need to sort out. I hope you'll give me a little time to do that.
>
> In the meantime, I'm going to take a short break from Capoeira. As much as I really, really want to continue training, I won't be able to sort much out if I have to see you every night in class with Bruna and everything.
>
> I hope you understand. Please be patient with me.
> Gabriela

She left the note on his coffee table, picked up her things and then let herself out of his apartment with tears once again, threatening to fall.

The sun streamed through the windows. As Sean slowly woke up, he automatically reached for Gabriela. He felt nothing. He tried to open his eyes and he winced against the brightness of the sun. He eventually got used to the light. There was no sign of her in his bedroom.

'Gaby.' His voice was croaky like a frog so he cleared his throat and tried again. 'Gabriela...'

There was still no response. He dragged his still-naked body out of bed, stretching his tired muscles as he stood up. He paused briefly to put on some boxers before he went looking for her. An empty living room greeted him as he entered it. A sinking feeling came over him and when he spied the note propped up on his coffee table, the feeling got even worse. He picked it up and read it slowly. With every sentence, he felt her slipping away. Sean wondered what he had expected. He was the one who had a baby on the way with another woman. How could he expect Gabriela to want to be saddled with this? They had known each other for a relatively short time, though he sometimes felt as if he'd known her forever. No woman had ever captivated him as much as Gabriela had. She was funny and engaging, and he had gotten used to having her in his life as well as being a part of the Capoeira school. He knew how much she'd grown to love it, and the last thing he wanted was for her to be deprived of training just because of his situation. So he found his phone and texted her.

> Sean: Hi Gaby. I understand. Trust me, I do. I don't want you to miss out on training because of this. I'm required to be there on Sun, Mon, Wed and Thurs, as I have to teach with *Escorpião*, so please go if you still want to

> on the other days. I'll stay away. You're a great capoeirista. The *batizado* is coming up soon, and I know how much you love training.
>
> I'm here whenever you're ready to talk.
>
> I'll miss you.

He knew he would miss seeing her all the time. But he would give her all the time she needed to clear her head. He himself still had a lot to figure out in regards to Bruna and the baby.

Sean put Gabriela's note back on the coffee table and went about preparing for his work day. There was no hope that this would be a good one.

Gabriela read his text while still lying in bed. She had tossed and turned and hadn't been able to sleep much since she got home. She knew she would miss him too, but for now, the separation was for the best.

As for training, it warmed her that he would make such a sacrifice in his own training just so she would feel comfortable going. As he said, the belt ceremony, or *batizado*, was coming up and she needed to train. *Mestre Escorpião* had already told her that she would be receiving her first belt, the green. She felt very proud of herself. It would be three days of specialised workshops, the ceremony itself and a big party. Masters and high-level students from all over Europe and Brazil would be coming to teach classes, impart their knowledge, put the students going up or receiving a belt through their paces and join in the celebrations. It promised to be a spectacular few days, and it would have been a shame not to be in her best shape for that.

In the meantime, she had to figure out what to do about the Bruna situation. Gabriela already decided that she would invite Tanya over later to help her figure all this out.

By evening time, Gabriela was even more confused than ever, so having Tanya agree to come over was just what she needed.

'She's pregnant!' Tanya was flabbergasted when Gabriela told her what had taken place. 'How in the hell did you manage to get yourself into this situation, Gaby?'

'I don't know. I don't know what to do.'

'Do you still want to be with him?'

Gabriela searched her heart before answering.

'Yes.'

'You've got it bad, huh?'

Gabriela nodded.

'You're in love with him, aren't you?'

Gabriela nodded again.

'Oh, honey.' Tanya gave her a hug. They were sitting on the sofa in Gabriela's living room, sipping on some wine. 'Have you told him how you feel?'

'Kind of.'

'What does that mean, "Kind of". Either you

told him or you didn't.'

'Well, I said it, but I'm not sure he heard me. A part of me is glad if he didn't.'

Tanya's expression showed that she was more than a little confused.

'How is it possible that you could have said something so important and he wouldn't have heard you? What else were you doing at the time?'

Gabriela's eyes opened wide and then she inclined her head, hoping that Tanya would get the message.

'You mean you were having...?'

Gabriela took a sip of her wine without answering.

'You were mid…?'

Then, another sip.

Tanya burst out laughing. 'You really know how to pick your moment, don't you, Gab?'

Gabriela couldn't help but laugh herself.

'So, what does he plan to do? Go back to this Bruna girl? Go old school and marry her?'

'No!' Gabriela's answered quickly. The truth is, she didn't know what he might do in this regard. He'd said that he had no intention of going back to Bruna. But you never know. He could change his mind at any time, and there was nothing that she could do about it.

'Are you sure about that?' Tanya probed.

'He said he didn't want to be in a relationship with her anymore but that he would support them and look after them both, as he should. He's a good man. But I don't know where I would fit into all of that. Having a child with someone is a big deal. They'll be a family.' Gabriela nearly choked on those last words.

'If he's a good man, then why won't you believe him when he tells you his romantic relationship with this woman is over? It sounds to me like you're the woman he wants to be with and that this was an accident that he wants to do his best to handle.'

'But Bruna says she wants him back.'

'She has a say in matters concerning the baby, naturally. Your boyfriend's love life is none of her business.'

'We haven't discussed titles.'

'That's irrelevant. It's clear to me that whatever is between you two, is far more than just casual.'

'I thought we were, but now everything feels uncertain.'

'And where did you leave things?'

'I told him I needed time.'

'You two need to keep talking.'

'I can't be around him right now. I'm afraid I'll agree to something just because I don't want to lose him.'

'The alternative would be to be without him.'

Gabriela, let what Tanya was saying sink in. She knew she wanted to be with him, but he still had a lot to figure out himself.

'I think he needs time too. He only just found out he's going to be a father. He's in more shock than I am. Don't you think the time apart would be good for us?'

'Perhaps. Just don't cut him off completely. Call him, text him, whatever. Just don't go into full incognito mode. Keep the lines of communication open so that while he's figuring out all this stuff, he knows what *all* of his options are. Okay?'

'Okay.' Talking to Tanya always helped to put things into perspective.

Gabriela had prepared dinner for her and Tanya, and as they sat and ate, she began to feel the clouds shifting. She still thought they both needed time to think, but Tanya had made her realise that she shouldn't cut him off completely. She resolved to call him later after Tanya left.

By eleven, Gabriela was alone, enjoying the last of her wine. She decided to take Tanya's advice and to keep the lines of communication open. So, she called Sean. After a couple of rings, the line connected.

'What do *you* want?'

The voice on the other end of the call was not that of the man she was in love with. She would recognise Bruna's accented tone anywhere.

That now familiar sickness started wreaking havoc again with Gabriela's stomach. She realised that her hands had started to shake. Why was Bruna answering Sean's phone. And if he was at home, what was she doing there this late. All manner of scenarios started crossing Gabriela's mind and none of them were particularly good.

'Can I speak to Sean, please?' To her own ears, Gabriela voice sounded alien.

'Why won't you leave my family and I alone? Don't you know when you're not wanted? Sean has more important things to think about right now than some silly girl and her *feelings*.'

Gabriela took a quick intake of breath. Bruna sounded so nasty and hateful. The last thing she wanted to do was to hear this woman voice, but she desperately need to talk to Sean.

'Who's that?'

This last voice sounded much further away, but it was unmistakably Sean's.

'No one important,' came the venomous voice of Bruna.

Then the line went dead.

Gabriela gripped her phone. Her head pounded. Operating only on autopilot, she squeezed the button on the side of her phone and then touched the screen, turning it off completely.

Sean walked into his living room, holding a cup of herbal tea for Bruna. He had invited her over so that they could talk about their situation and come up with a plan of action moving forward. There was a child on the way, and he would do the best that he could for both mother and child.

As he entered, he saw Bruna with his phone to her ear.

'Who's that?' He asked.

Bruna shrugged her shoulders. 'No one important.'

He saw the glint in her eyes and then suddenly had a sinking feeling in his gut. He put the tea down on the coffee table and then took his phone out of Bruna's grip. He quickly reviewed his call history and saw who the last caller was. He only barely held back the expletives that came to his mind.

'What did you say to her?' Sean was furious, but he knew losing his temper wouldn't do any good.

'Nothing. I just told her the truth. It's not my fault if she didn't want to hear it.'

'Bruna—' He stopped himself before he said something out of anger. 'Please, be careful how you speak to and about Gabriela.'

'Why should I?'

'She's in my life.' Sean suppressed the thought that immediately came to his mind in regards to the 'time' Gabriela had asked for. The fact that she'd tried to call him must mean that she was reaching out. This is something that he was grateful for. But as Bruna had answered his phone, and Lord knows what she'd actually said to her, who knows what Gabriela was thinking about him right now. He knew he needed to call her back as soon as possible.

'*I'm* in your life! And soon, there will be two of us.'

He bowed his head. 'I know. And I'll take my responsibility as a father seriously. But nothing is going to change the fact that after you cheated on me, I moved on with my life. Gabriela is now a part of that.

Bruna rolled her eyes and started grabbing her handbag.

'You need to get your priorities straight, Sean.'

With a slam of his door, she was gone. Sean exhaled. Without a doubt, in the last few days, his life had become extremely complicated.

He brought up Gabriela's name again on his phone so that he could call her back. It went straight to voicemail, her beautiful voice telling him that she was unavailable. His brow wrinkled. He repeated his actions and once again it immediately went to voicemail.

She switched off her phone!

Undoubtedly. Whatever Bruna had said to her must have upset her so much, that she'd switched off her phone.

'Fuck!'

There was no reason not to let out the expletive now.

What must she be thinking?

He didn't have a clue as to when he would see or hear from Gabriela again, but knowing that she was reaching out to him this soon made him feel good. But now...

'Dammit, Bruna!'

A few days had passed since she'd tried to call him and had gotten Bruna instead. She'd seen his missed calls and heard his voice messages asking her to call him back, but she'd ignored all of it. The perspective she'd gained after Tanya's visit was gone, and she was back to being confused and frustrated. She needed to find a way to get rid of this negative energy.

This is how she'd ended up dressed in all whites that Saturday night, positioned at the *atabaque,* getting ready to play it for the *roda.* *Mestre Escorpião* sang the introduction *ladainha* and a couple of other songs, then he indicated that she should sing the next song. This would be her very first time singing lead. She was nervous, but a part of her was excited too.

Gabriela matched her drumbeat with the rhythm of the *berimbau* and the *pandeiro*, and then she began her song.

Avisa meu mano,
Avisa meu mano,
Avisa meu mano,
Capoeira mandou me chamar

Capoeira é luta nossa, da era colonial
E nasceu foi na Bahia, Angola e Regional

This was the first of three songs she sang. There was something thrilling, cleansing and soul defining about singing the music of Capoeira. This was the exact release that she had needed. It was strange being there without Sean. She could feel him everywhere in this space. But it was also nice to experience Capoeira on her own terms without Bruna presence mocking her.

She also played a few times and that added to her good vibes for the night. The cherry on top was when *Mestre Escorpião* came to her at the end of the class.

'Gabriela, you nickname will be *Canora*, alright?'

That's all he said before he walked away.

Canora... singer.

She smiled.

When Gabriela went to grab her bag, Jennifer and Oksana came up to her.

'Hey! We heard the news,' Jennifer said

When Gabriela gave her a puzzled look, she continued.

'Bruna's been going around telling people at the office and here too that she's pregnant for her *boyfriend*, Sean.'

Gabriela's calm at having such a wonderful lesson and being given her special Capoeira nickname, started to evaporate.

'Is it true? I'm so sorry. We heard Sean only recently found out about it.'

'Um... yes.'

Then Oksana chimed in. 'I can't believe she's that far along and she waited all this time before she told him.'

'What is it? Over four months, right?' Jennifer asked.

'It appears to be four and a half months, yes.' Gabriela did not want to talk about Bruna, but she didn't want to be rude either, as she really liked Jennifer and Oksana.

'I remember back then. She went back to Brazil for like a month,' Oksana said.

'Then, when she came back, I caught her screwing one of our work colleagues at the office post-Christmas party. It made me wonder how long that was going on. I don't know what Sean saw in her.'

Gabriela remembered that Sean had told her that it was Jennifer who'd told him what Bruna had done.

'So, are you and Sean going to split up?' Jennifer enquired. 'You're far better for him than she could ever be.'

Gabriela knew that Jennifer and Sean were good friends, but she did not feel quite as comfortable sharing the details of her and Sean's relationship with anyone at the school. She doubted Sean would want that either. At least not until the two of them figured out what they were going to do.

'We're playing it by ear for now.'

The girls thankfully backed off then, and they all went to get changed. Jennifer and Oksana wanted to hang back in the Centre for some reason, but Gabriela didn't question it. She was more than happy to be alone right now and head home. She exited the building and then headed to the location where she and Sean would park their cars.

As she rounded the corner, she saw her car, and something else too. Or, *someone* else, to be exact. All six feet tall and drop-dead gorgeousness of Sean Lancaster was propped against the driver's side door of her car.

Almost immediately, her heart went into overdrive. It had been days since she had last seen him. The inner Gabriela wanted to run to reach him faster and plant kisses all over his handsome face. But, of course, she did not. She took a deep breath and kept walking at her normal pace. As she got closer, she saw stress and strain written all over his face. One side of his mouth lifted in a smile.

'Hi.'

'Sean...' Despite what she had told him about needing time, she was very, very happy to see him. She dropped her gym bag and gave him a hug. He followed suit and embraced her too. He smelled good. She had missed that scent so much.

'How did you know I was here?' She said as she lifted her head away from his chest to look into his eyes.

'A little birdie told me?' Sean said with a wink.

At first, Gabriela didn't know what he was alluding to, but then she understood.

'Jennifer!'

Sean smiled cheekily, indicating that she had guessed right.

She giggled, shook her head, and then once again, placed it on Sean's chest. It felt right being where she was.

She could hear his heartbeat. It was strong and faster than she would normally expect it to be. She knew that he must be feeling a lot of what she was. Plus, he must have been annoyed that she'd been avoiding his calls since the night Bruna had answered his phone. She just couldn't face it all. She knew that she was a chicken for not dealing with all of this head-on, but it seemed so much easier, for now, to just pretend that the man she was in love with wasn't having a child with another woman.

'Weren't you supposed to be giving me time?' She reluctantly pulled herself away from him and put her bag in the trunk of her car.

He gave her a sheepish grin. 'I was planning to, but then you stopped answering my messages. I wanted to make sure you were alright and to apologise.'

'Apologise for what?'

'For whatever it was that Bruna said to you when she answered my phone.'

'Oh, that.' Gabriela didn't really want to be reminded of that.

'Can we go someplace quiet and talk?'

She nodded.

When she locked her car, he held his hand out to her. She put her hand in his, and then he lifted her hand to his lips and kissed it. His breath was warm on her skin, and it sent tingles up her spine.

They walked up the street to a small pub that she'd seen before, but had never gone into. It wasn't particularly loud or busy. Sean ordered them a couple of drinks at the bar, and then they found a secluded booth at the back.

As soon as they sat down, Sean pulled her close to him and kissed her on the lips. It was all too brief for Gabriela's liking, but it was nice feeling this close to him again. Sean took a swig of his scotch before he spoke.

'First of all, I wanted to say that Bruna only answered my phone because she was at my place so we could discuss a plan moving forward with the baby. I left the room to make her some tea, and I guess that's the same time that you called. Nothing happened between us.'

It felt good that he wanted to make sure she understood.

'I know nothing happened.'

'How do you know?'

'Because I trust you.' This was a fact that Gabriela was clear about above almost anything. Even though they had not talked about any titles or defined their relationship, she knew that she could trust him, regardless of the doubts that sometimes crept in.

He smiled and gave her hand a squeeze. 'Thank you for trusting me.'

'Of course. I told her I want to be hands-on, check-ups, feedings, nappies, the works. It's going to mean big changes for me, my lifestyle... and for us.' Sean looked away from her, a shadow crossing his face. 'That is, if you want there to be an "*us*".'

Gabriela mulled that word over in her mind. Was she willing to jump head first into a much more complicated relationship than she had started to imagine for them?

'I'm not naïve. I know that this is going to be tough. Your child will have to come first, and the time we can spend together will be impacted by this. I don't know how I will feel or deal with it down the line, but...' She took a deep breath. This was a huge step for her. 'I... I'd like to try.'

He looked deep into her eyes.

'Are you sure, Gaby? I don't want you to do or say anything just to make me feel better.'

'No, that's not it. I'm saying all of this for me. I don't know if we have a chance. This situation might be too big for "*us*" to survive. But we won't know until we have a go.'

He smiled. It was a broad smile that reflected in his eyes.

'You're amazing, you know that?' He pulled her close, and with his lips next to her ear, he said, 'You know I'm crazy about you, right?'

Gabriela's heartbeat quickened.

He went on, pulling away a little so he could look her in the eyes. 'I think there was something between us from the moment I caught you spying on me.'

She laughed. 'You're never going to let that one go, are you?'

'Not in this lifetime.' They both enjoyed the joke, then his face sobered. 'Gabriela.'

'Yes.'

'I love you.'

Her eyes widened in shock. That is not what she'd thought he was about to say. Her heart beat wildly in her chest and tears came to her eyes. She lowered her head and shook it, but he misunderstood her actions.

'I'm sorry if that's not something you want to hear. I just needed to tell you, even if you don't feel the same.'

She looked up at him quickly. 'No, no, I do. What I mean is. I did want to hear that. Or I do.' She was rambling. She took a breath. 'Sean, I love you too. More than anything.'

There was silence between them for a moment while what they'd just admitted to each other sank in.

When their lips met, it was in celebration of what they knew they meant to each other and the promise that they hoped the future held.

Against her lips, he said, 'Let's get out of here.'

They left the table with their drinks as yet unfinished and headed for the door. They walked back and got into their respective cars. As Gabriela guided her car through London traffic, she glanced multiple times into her rear-view mirror. Sean followed behind her at every turn. A surge of excitement surged through Gabriela. Knowing that the man she loved, loved her right back, had her on cloud nine.

CHAPTER 12

- bateria -

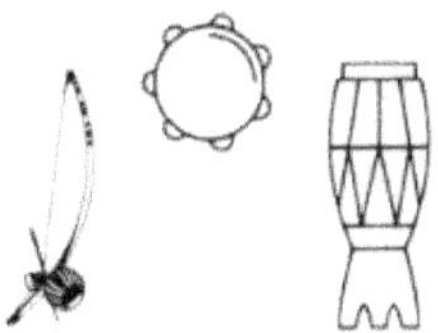

In the weeks that followed, Sean and Gabriela went back to training together and preparations were underway for the workshops and *batizado*. She finally felt secure in the love that she and Sean shared and the barbs that Bruna sent her way no longer had an impact on her.

On the first day of the event, Gabriela was so excited. The visitors to their school were so interesting to meet. She struck up a conversation in Spanish with a *Contramestre*, which was the Capoeira rank just below master, from Spain. His name was Javier Martínez. He had a vineyard in the north of Spain, and that was very much the vein in which their conversation went on. Gabriela loved her wine and loved trying out different grapes from around the world. She'd never tried the wine, *Ribera del Duero*, from his particular region before, but by the way he had described it, she'd been intrigued.

'My late wife, Isabel, had a passion for wine and we often argued into the night about what was best for our vines.' He had a wistful look on his face as he mentioned her.

Gabriela felt very sad about his loss.

'My condolences, Javier.'

'It is alright, *amiga*. She still lives on in me.'

'When did she pass?'

For a split second, she saw a deep sadness in his eyes.

'It will be a year in a few days.'

On instinct, she reached out and gave him a reassuring pat on the arm.

'Anyway, today is a celebration.' A smile came back to his face. 'You will receive your first belt today, yes?'

'*¡Sí! Mestre Escorpião* has been a great teacher. I feel very honoured.'

'I'm sure you have worked very hard for it.'

'*Contramestre Incêndio*!' A shout came from somewhere across the room.

Javier's eyes sought out the person who had called his nickname from somewhere in room full of capoeiristas. He was being summoned by another one of the visitors. Javier indicated with a nod that he'd heard the man. He turned back to her and gave her an apologetic look.

'It seems I must go.'

Gabriela nodded. *'Qué significa "Incêndio"?'* She had picked up a lot of Portuguese so far, but *"Incêndio"* was a word she wanted to clarify.

'It means "Fire". Gabriela, *amiga*, it was very nice to meet you. I'm sure we will talk again during the festivities.'

'¡*Encantada*!'

And it *was* nice to meet him. He seemed like a nice man, and Gabriela was looking forward to taking the workshop he would be teaching shortly.

She was about to go off and search for Sean when someone grabbed her arm. It was Jennifer. Her face was red with something akin to panic.

'Jennifer, are you alright?'

'Yes! I mean, no! Where is Sean? I have something to tell him and it can't wait.'

Gabriela's alarm bells went off immediately.

'I'm not sure where he is. I was just about to look for him. She looked around the room. They were using an additional, much bigger studio in the Sports Centre for the three days of events. Multiple workshops would take place there as well as in the regular studio next door. Sean was probably in there.

'He could be next door. Do you want me to go get him?'

'No!'

It was almost a snap. And immediately, Jennifer's face showed that she regretted the sharpness of her tone.

'No. I need to talk to Sean first. I'm positive he will want to fill you in later.'

Gabriela nodded, feeling a sudden sense of anxiety about whatever it was that Jennifer needed to speak to Sean about.

Jennifer then quickly hurried out of the room.

'Okay guys, get into your groups for the workshops you selected to do.'

Mestre Escorpião was ready to begin the first of the workshops.

Finding out what had Jennifer so panicked would have to wait. Gabriela headed in the direction of the group that would be led by Gabriela's new friend, Javier.

Sean was chatting at the back of their regular studio with one of the visiting *Professores* from Brazil. As Sean was fluent in Portuguese, and had been for a number of years, they communicated in this language.

'*Oi Raposo! Como vai você?*' *Professor Pão* greeted Sean.

'Everything's good, you know.' Sean wasn't just saying that to be polite. He felt happy.

'Thanks for offering your hotel to us again this year. We always appreciate your generosity.'

Sean put his right palm on over his heart. 'It's my pleasure.'

Out of the corner of his eye, Sean saw Jennifer come bursting into the room. She zeroed in on him and headed straight over.

What is it now?

'Sean! I need to talk to you. It's an emergency!'

Sean turned back to *Professor Pão*. 'My apologies.'

'No problem at all. *Adeus.*'

Sean turned to Jennifer.

'Not here. We need more privacy,' she said.

Jennifer turned and led Sean out into the hall and didn't start explaining until she found an empty room.

'I need to tell you something about Bruna.'

Sean shook his head. 'What has she done now?'

'Before I left the office today, I overheard her in a room talking to someone. It was to our co-worker whom I caught screwing her at the Christmas party. They were having an argument. He was saying that he heard she was pregnant.'

Sean's eyes narrowed at the mention of Bruna's pregnancy.

'He asked her how far along she was, and she said four and a half months.'

'She said what?' Sean's temper flared in an instant.

'She told him she was only four and a half months pregnant. But I know she should be closer to five and a half months by now. And if that's true, then it means she is lying to you.'

Sean paced up and down in the room. He suddenly felt like his head was splitting. None of this made sense.

'There's more.'

He swung around and looked at her.

'When he said that the baby was his, she told him that it was not. She said the baby already had a father.'

Sean's eyes were pure fury now.

'She told him if he dared to try to claim fatherhood of her child to anyone, she would ruin his marriage and his career.'

'Are you sure you heard all of this right? '

'I'm positive. She told him her doctor confirmed how far along she was.' Jennifer took a long deep breath. 'The baby is not yours, Sean.'

He closed his eyes for a long time. When he opened them again, he simply took out his phone and started dialling.

It was a video call, as he wanted to see her eyes. When Bruna finally answered, Sean did his best to keep his temper in check.

'Sean!' Bruna smiled. 'I can't come to the *batizado* today, but I will be at the workshops tomorrow.'

'Don't bother.' At Sean's tone, Bruna's expression changed. 'Is it true?'

'Is what true?'

'That you deceived me? That the child is not mine?

Bruna's eyes opened wide. 'Who told you that?'

'Never mind who told me. Is it true? Did you try to pawn off another man's child as mine?'

'I... I can't believe you'd ever... think I'd do that.'

'I believe you're capable of many things Bruna. And whether you tell me now or a doctor confirms it after the child is born, I *will* find out.'

Bruna's jaw tightened.

'*Fine*!' The confession was not given with any kind of pleasure. 'It's true. The baby is not yours. But it could be, Sean. We could raise this child together. Don't you want that?'

'What I *wanted* was the truth. Tell me something, Bruna. What were you planning to do when the child didn't arrive when, as far as I knew, it should?'

'I hoped, by then, you wouldn't care.'

'Listen to me, and listen to me carefully. I never, ever, want to see you again.'

'Sean, I—'

He cut the call. He didn't want to hear any more of her lies.

He took a deep breath and let it out slowly. Then he turned and looked at Jennifer, who was still there.

'Thank you...' The relief and something else he could not quite yet identify in his voice, were palpable. '...again.'

'What are friends for!'

◆ ◆ ◆

It was so thrilling being among such talented capoeiristas. In many ways, their playing styles differed from *Jogo Arrepiado Capoeira*. But at their heart, everyone present was committed to this discipline that was Capoeira.

The workshops that evening were so amazing and she felt she was learning so much. She hadn't seen Sean most of the evening as he was in the other studio. Now that they had a break before the *batizado* itself started, she went to find him. She felt anxiety for whatever it was Jennifer had had to say to him.

She eventually found him near the main entrance. He greeted her with a smile, but she could see that something was bothering him.

'What's wrong? What did Jennifer say?'

He embraced her, holding her close and not saying a word for a while. Then he pulled back a little.

'I love you, Gaby. Don't ever forget that.'

'I love you too, honey.' She touched his cheek and gave him a peck on the lips. 'Please tell me what happened.'

Sean recounted what Jennifer told him, and then what Bruna had in turn said to him herself.

'I can't believe she would do something like that.' Gabriela was in shock.

'Believe it.' His words held a sharp edge.

'My heart is breaking for you Sean.'

'Why?' He shrugged. 'I finally know the truth.'

'Because you thought you were going to be a father in a few months.'

He closed his eyes and dropped his head. When he opened them again, Gabriela could see that what he had learned was haunting him.

He said, 'We will deal with that later. For now, this is your night. Let's go to the *batizado.*

The ceremony was fantastic. All the students receiving a new belt had to play with an upper-level capoeirista from their school or one of the visitors in one giant *roda*. Gabriela and the others' skills were tested, and a few of them even ended up on their butts.

Then, one by one, they were called up, given a certificate and their belts. She was beaming and excited after she received hers. She made her way over to Sean. He gave her a congratulatory hug. She knew he was happy for her. He took her brand new green belt, wound it through the loops on her white trousers and showed her how to secure it. She had to admit, she felt proud of herself.

When the event started winding down, they said their goodbyes to everyone. They declined the invitations to the pub that everyone kept giving them, promising that they would join everyone for the celebrations after the workshops the following day. They both knew that tonight, too much had been found out for them to really be in the mood to join everyone.

◆ ◆ ◆

Later, as they lay in bed at her house, Jennifer's revelation played through both of their minds.

'Gabriela, you're the best thing that's ever happened to me, and I'm very happy you're a terrible spy.'

They both burst out laughing. The joke loosened the tension, and they were finally able to relax.

He reached for her and kissed her. It was a long and tender kiss, one which lit a familiar flame inside her. He cupped her breast through her lacy nightie and squeezed gently on her now pert nipples. She let out a soft yelp at the pleasure it gave her. Then he moved his lips to where his fingers had been. She closed her eyes and savoured the torrent of emotions that were now flowing through her.

Gabriela stroked his rock-hard erection and it sent spasm through his core.

'I want you, baby. I *need* you now!' She almost begged.

Sean smiled wickedly, 'I'm here for your pleasure, milady.'

He lifted himself above her and just before his tip penetrated her, he took her lips in a mind-blowing kiss which seared her senses and threatened to push her over the edge. When he drove into her, she groaned out his name. This only spurred him on. Using one of her legs as leverage, he anchored himself with it, and continued to thunder into her.

The connection between them was strong. It was both physical and emotional. Nothing and no one could ever get in the way of that. They knew this instinctively.

They didn't take their eyes off each other until they'd both gone over the edge and collapsed in a heap. They took ragged breaths as they came down from their highs.

They continued to make love until well into the night, worshiping each other's body in ways they hadn't done before. From the moment they'd first met, there was a spark that had been ignited inside of them. A flame which had grown exponentially, which now fused them together.

'I love you, Gaby.' She heard him whisper this into her ear as they were both falling asleep, exhausted by their exploits.

The last thing she was aware of before she slipped into slumber was the feeling of pure, unadulterated happiness and love.

LEAVE A REVIEW

I would be truly grateful if you would leave a review!

Leaving a positive review is like a blessing for up and coming authors like myself and helps others to engage with our work. Also, if we know what our readers want, we can provide it.

I would be truly touched to hear from my readers!

Thank you!

amazon

Click to Review

ABOUT THE AUTHOR

Shonel Jackson

Shonel is originally from Guyana in South America. She moved to London as a teenager. She's a creative by nature and has been a professional actress, poet, an English as a foreign teacher and jewellery design/ maker.

She fell in love with romance novels as a teenager. Throughout her life, she's consumed them ravenously. She started writing her own a few years after reading her first. Nothing could stop her after that.

She loves to write strong female leads, primarily women of colour. Her ladies are vibrant, worldly and not afraid of a challenge. Her guys are irresistible and smouldering and will stop at nothing to win their prize.

You'll laugh, maybe shed a little tear and drown in the worlds she likes to weave.

BOOKS IN THIS SERIES

Era Capoeira

Enter the world of Capoeira! This is a multi-faceted martial art, dance, sport and game from Brazil. It attracts people who are just looking for something... more.

The main setting is the Jogo Arrepiado Capoeira school in the centre of London. In this Era Capoeira Series, you will meet people who have found Capoeira through various means, who've become hooked on it and those relationships which blossom in it's midst.

Let's Play

Gabriela Espinosa is no 007!

Let's get that straight! What she is, is the owner of La Duquesa, a high end night club in the Centre of London. In Book 1 of the Era Capoeira Series, she meets a man one night who will ignite her passions. The meeting happens quite by accident... because she is spying! As LET'S PLAY begins, Gabriela is called by the rich, often sensual music of Capoeira. If she hadn't been in the right place at the right time, they might never have met. But from the moment they first lay eyes on each other, the spell was cast...

Sean Lancaster is a successful hotelier in the prime of his life. His business is growing leaps and bounds and his life has been enriched by Capoeira, a martial art which he has loved since he was a teenager. He has no complaints. But one night, a chance encounter with a stunningly intoxicating woman has Sean realising that maybe there is something missing in his perfect life.

He just had to hope that after he gives her a business card, she actually contacts him.

Playing With Fire

In Playing With Fire, Book 2 of the martial arts series, Era Capoeira, we meet Javier Martínez and Luna Michaels. Their story begins with a one night stand. The connection between them is instantaneous. One look into her golden-brown eyes and Javier is hooked. The problem was that he had no business being attracted to Luna or any other woman for that matter, right now. His trip to

London was supposed to be a short one. Javier's life at home in Spain and the past he was still dealing with, ensured that he would stick to that plan.

Luna had been to many of the Capoeira workshops at the school she'd been a part of for years. They were the highlight of the season and she always looked forward to them. This year, however, she meets one particular invitee, who she simply cannot resist, nor does she want to.

When their one night of passion comes to an end, Javier walks away from it feeling guilt-ridden, and Luna, with a little surprise.

Outplayed

Book 3 of 3, OUTPLAYED, will follow in 2023. The series concludes with Dominic and Willow "the Viper's" story.

'PLAYING WITH FIRE' REVIEWS

Mylene, Amazon UK Review (6th December, 2022)
★★★★★
Oh, what a night! Javier and Luna meet up again after a few years but they are very different people this time. Is forgiveness on the cards for these two? And is it allowed?

CLorraine Kibler, Goodreads Review (10 November, 2022)
★★★★★
I thoroughly enjoyed this international love story and look forward eagerly to the next instalment.

Manisha Robinson, Goodreads Review (11th November, 2022)
★★★★★
This is book two in the Era Capoeira Series. This story is an instalove interracial steamy

erotic contemporary romance. The characters are loveable with great chemistry and a happy ending.

Jenita Zellar (28th October, 2022)
★★★★
First book I've read by this author and I'm glad I ran across it. It's a very good book. The characters were strong and the story had a very good flow. I definitely recommend it to all those hopeless romantics out there…me included.

'PLAYING WITH FIRE' EXTRACT

Swipe to see an extract from
PLAYING WITH FIRE (Era Capoeira, Book 2)

PROLOGUE

- ginga -

Javier Martínez hadn't attended another Capoeira school's *batizado*, or belt giving celebrations, in over a year, let alone one outside of Spain. Ever since his dear wife Isabel had passed, he had lost interest in many things, including the Brazilian martial art which had long been a part of his life. It had taken a gargantuan effort from Fabian, his most senior student, to get him to accept *Mestre Escorpião's* invitation to fly to London and participate in the *Jogo Arrepiado Capoeira* school's *batizado* celebrations. For almost a year, he had entrusted his school to Fabian. He couldn't bring himself to feel the inevitable comfort that playing Capoeira would bring again. This had been his self-imposed exile from the game since Isabel's death.

Capoeira had been fundamental to his life, almost all of his life. Over the years, he had progressed to the level of *Contramestre*, one level below Master or *Mestre*, as they said amongst each other. He'd had three loves in life. One was Capoeira. Another was producing the finest wines at his vineyard in the north of Spain. The final and most important had been Isabel. They'd both come from wine producing families who'd been close friends for generations. It had become almost a foregone conclusion that Javier and Isabel would marry one day. Their union was an easy one. She was sweet and loving and he cherished her. Then one day, in an instant, she was gone.

Now, almost a year since that fateful day, he was driving a rental car, heading to the Capoeira *batizado* celebrations of his friend, João da Costa or *Mestre Escorpião*, as he was known in the Capoeira world.

'*Mestre Escorpião*', translated to Master Scorpion. The majority of people who practised, or 'played' Capoeira, which was the word used amongst capoeiristas to describe what they did, had a special Capoeira nickname. It was usually given to them by the master of the school they attended. The nickname was often based on the person's personality, features or some abstract quality that the master saw in them.

This was Javier's first time visiting *Escorpião's* school. With the anniversary of his wife's death fast approaching, he had originally only planned to spend this time alone, with only his grief for company. But now that he was here, seeing the people walking around this Sports Centre that was buzzing with the energy only Capoeira had the power to bring, something which had been dormant in him started to stir again.

After he got changed into his white *abadas*, or Capoeira trousers, and t-shirt, he went in search of his friend, the school's master. When he realised he wasn't having much luck in his quest, he decided to ask someone. Just ahead of him in the corridor was a woman, who, by her outfit, was a capoeirista too.

'*Oi!* Do you know where I can find *Mestre Escorpião*?'

The woman stopped and turned around. She gave him a beaming smile in acknowledgement of his question. Javier cocked his head a little to the side as he observed her. She was relatively tall, with slender curves and a knockout smile.

¡Dios! Where did that come from?

It had been a while since any other woman had piqued his interest in any way, shape or form. But there was something about this woman. Something he couldn't quite put his finger on.

Her dark, curly hair was swept up in a ponytail, likely in preparation for the evening of workshops ahead. He started to wonder what it would be like if all of her hair was allowed to cascade around her face or if it was splayed across his pillow.

¡Dios mío, Javier! What the hell has got into you?

Her caramel skin looked soft and inviting.

And those eyes!

Those must be her best, most beautiful features. His eyes narrowed as he got totally sucked into their golden-brown depths.

Her lips were moving and a part of him knew that she had just said something, but for the life of him, he had no idea what it was.

She snapped her fingers in his face. 'Hey! Are

you feeling alright?'

This, thankfully, did make him snap out of it.

'What did you say?' He asked, feeling slightly embarrassed by the fact that he was behaving like an infatuated schoolboy.

A look of concern now replaced her smile.

'I said, *Mestre* is in the large studio over there. But you looked like you were someplace else for a second there,' she said.

He shook his head to make sure the last of his daydream was gone.

'I'm fine, *gracias*. Which way?'

'I'm heading that way too, so you can come with me.'

'*Perfecto*. Lead the way.'

As he walked next to her, he could smell the subtle scent of her perfume. It was intoxicating.

'So, which school are you from?' She asked curiously.

'*Capoeira Balança,* in Spain.'

'Oh, that's great. I've been to Spain, but just for a little holiday.'

Her smile was back again and he once again noted her mesmerising eyes as she glanced at him.

'Really? Where did you visit?'

'Oh, it was just a girlie getaway in Mallorca. Fun in the sun, you know.'

'Ah, yes,' he smiled. 'I have heard of these... what do you call it... "*girlie getaways*".'

'By the way, thanks so much for coming and being a part of our *batizado* and workshops.'

Javier found the sound of her voice enthralling. They reached a door and he followed her through.

'There he is over there,' she said, indicating by pointing in the *Mestre's* direction.

'*Gracias,* ah...'

'Oh yes, sorry. I'm Luna.'

'*Gracias*, Luna.'

'You're welcome, ah...'

'Javier, but most of my friends call me Javi.'

There was a glint in her eyes and she had a much more sensual tone to her voice as she spoke again.

'So, what should *I* call you?'

'Javi, of course.'

Javier could barely believe it. He was flirting! As soon as the thought crossed his mind, he felt a pang of guilt. He realised he needed to get away from this woman. This... *Luna*...

He cleared his throat, ended their eye contact and then spoke gruffly.

'Anyway, enjoy the festivities.' Then he walked off. He knew that might have come off rude, but he couldn't stay there while being sucked into those golden brown depths.

Luna thoroughly enjoyed this season's *batizado*

and workshops. It was always good to see the newer students receiving their first belts or the more seasoned ones going up a level. It was an event to celebrate.

For this *batizado*, something else entirely had also stood out. It was *Contramestre Incêndio… Contramestre* Fire… Javier… Javi…

It should be a sin to be as sexy as that man is!

During the meet-and-greet, before the start of the first workshop, she had been chatting with her good friend Oksana as she covertly watched him in a conversation with Gabriela, the girlfriend of *Instrutor Raposo*, Instructor Fox. She wished she could come up with a plausible excuse to go over and talk to him again, but at that moment, she couldn't think of one.

Though she had enjoyed the entire weekend of excitement, she still hadn't bucked up her courage to go over and talk to him again.

Now, at the party on the final night, with a glass of liquid courage in her hand and a fair amount of it in her system, she approached him. They had reserved the room above a busy bar for the party. Everyone up there was either from her school or a visiting capoeirista from the U.K. or internationally.

Tonight, she had opted for a short, strappy blue dress. She let her curls fly free and wore minimal makeup, as she always did.

When she reached him, she touched his arm

to get his attention. He turned around and immediately, she was hit by his sheer magnetism.

It's a sin... an absolute sin!

'Luna!' He smiled.

'You remembered,' she said breathlessly.

'Of course. I was beginning to think my entire visit would pass before you would speak to me again.'

Luna was surprised. 'You wanted to speak to me?'

'Yes. You intrigue me.'

His accent and his smile were doing strange things to her insides.

'Do I?' She asked coyly.

'I wish I could show you how much.' He leaned over and whispered this in her ear.

Her pulse rate sped up and she could feel herself getting hot, but it had nothing to do with the room being full of people. Just *one* of those people.

Her newfound courage had her saying, 'I wish you could show me too.'

Her invitation, and it *was* an invitation, hung in the air, neither of them looking away from the other. They silently communicated everything that needed to be said. He took her hand, led her downstairs and out of the front door.

'My hotel is only five minute walk from here,' he said, his voice sounding gruff and sensual at the same time.

She walked with him, her hand in his, anticipation bubbling up inside her. Once they entered his room, he had her out of her dress in no time.

She frantically tried to unbutton his shirt as he claimed her mouth with a kiss. When the buttons started getting the better of her, she ripped open the shirt out of frustration, sending the offending fasteners flying across the room. With his shirt discarded, she went for his belt buckle. Before she could finish her task, he scooped her up in his arms and placed her on the king-sized bed with her legs hanging off the side. He got on his knees beside the bed, spreading her legs and then he took her with his tongue. He licked the most sensitive part of her as she writhed around on the bed, feeling like she was about to burst.

This was a first for Luna. She'd barely had one full conversation with this man, but Javier set her pulse racing unlike any other man, and she could not keep her hands off him. She groaned as he took her to new heights and when she thought she could take it no longer, she felt her body tense and then release in spasms.

He stood and finished off what she had started with his belt buckle. When he'd fully undressed, he stood before her erect, ready to complete his conquest.

He frowned, '*Cara*, I was not prepared for anything like this when I left Spain. Please tell me you are protected.' His words were ragged and full of unabridged need.

'I'm on the pill and otherwise safe. What about you?' she asked.

'Well, I'm *not* on the pill, but I am safe.' That brought a glint to his eye and she giggled at his joke.

He entered her swiftly, driving deep. The need she felt for this man she barely knew was astronomical.

'What do you want, *cara*?'

'*You*, Javi.'

That brought a wicked smile to his face as he increased his rhythm until, with a ragged exhale, he released his seed. His eyes closed as he rode the wave, eventually bringing his full weight down on her. He was heavy, but not unpleasantly so.

'Luna, what have you done to me?'

'What do you mean?'

'It's been a while since I've tried this hard to get near any woman, only to have her spend the same amount of time trying to avoid me. Then when she finally decides to come near me, I lose all sense and control.' He slowly eased himself out of her and collapsed by her side.

Luna didn't quite know what to say to all of that. What she did know was that this man had ignited something inside of her which was unlikely to go away anytime soon.

'But don't worry, *guapa*, it will be even better next time.'

'Next time?' She was giddy with excitement to have more of him.

'We're not finished yet, Luna. I'm still intrigued,' he said as a sly smile creased his face.

Then he kissed her again and they spent the next long while trying to get whatever it was that had drawn them to each other out of their system.

◆ ◆ ◆

The next morning, Luna awoke feeling sated. She could not see Javier but could hear him in the en-suite. When he returned to the room, he was fully dressed in a business suit.

'You're awake.' His smile was a lot less relaxed than it had been last night. If Luna didn't know any better, she would have sworn he was trying not to meet her eyes.

'Yes… I am.'

'I'm leaving for the airport now. I have an early flight.'

'Oh. I'll get going then.' She started getting out of bed, casting her eyes around the room looking for her clothes. She spotted them folded on a chair nearby.

'There's no need to leave on my account. You can stay as long as you want to today. You can go back to sleep if you like.' His voice was clipped.

This was clearly not the same Javi with whom she had entered this hotel room last night.

'That's ok. I'd rather get home,' she said as she shuffled off of the bed, keeping the sheet tightly wrapped around her body.

'I'll let you get dressed then.' There was a rough edge to his voice.

He had vanished from the room before she could look up and watch him leave. Gone was the Javi who had driven her wild with lust last night. Today it was a much more serious Javier who could barely look at her. She got into her clothes as quickly as she could and then called a taxi.

She felt at a disadvantage when she entered the living area of the hotel suite as she was still in her skimpy dress from the night before and he was fully dressed, looking more like a serious businessman more than anything else.

'Well, I have a taxi coming. I'll get out of your way.' She said as she headed for the door.

Before she could reach it, he called out to her.

'Luna!'

She turned back to him as he approached her.

'I can't say I know what the protocol is here, but I did enjoy myself last night.'

It sounded like the words were being ripped from him. Even though he was trying his best to smile as he spoke, it was obvious that it did not reach his eyes. Something was definitely bothering him, maybe even about last night. She knew she'd better go before she overstayed her welcome.

'Yeah, me too.' It was the truth, but she didn't feel like dwelling on it in that moment.

He reached into his pocket, took out a card and handed it to her. She took it.

'In case you ever need anything,' he said.

'It was very nice meeting you, Javi…' She consulted the card. 'Javier Martínez… from Spain.'

'You too, Luna…'

'Michaels. Luna Michaels… from London.'

With nothing else keeping her there, she opened the door and pulled it closed behind her.

What Luna did not see was the haunted looked that crossed Javier's face as he watched her retreat out the door.

CHAPTER 1

- pião de mão -

Two years later

When Javier received an email from his old friend João da Costa for the third year in a row inviting him to London to take part in his school, *Jogo Arrepiado Capoeira's batizado*, he had felt a surge of excitement. However, even though he had sent an R.S.V.P. in the affirmative, there was still a part of him which had a tinge of nervousness about coming here again. The first time he'd been here was the last and only he'd been here. His first visit two years ago marked his first return to the sport he loved so much, but hadn't taken part in since his wife Isabel's death, nearly a year before that. He had been a shell of himself for a long while before coming to London then. But, it was more than just Capoeira which had reignited his fire for living.

He had met an intriguingly beautiful woman called Luna Michaels who had sparked his long dormant libido. Ever since Isabel's passing, he felt at times like parts of him had disappeared. He removed himself from the social scene, from his own Capoeira school, his vineyard, from women, from everything. He simply lost interest in anything that used to bring him any joy.

Then, he'd met Luna and a part of him had shifted a little. Still, it was more of a shift than anyone else in his life had been able to achieve with him in a long while. Upon his return to Spain after they'd slept together, he was consumed by guilt. It had happened just a few short days before the first anniversary of Isabel's death. He felt that he'd betrayed her memory and he'd spent a lot of time hating himself and his weakness. This is why he had not come again to the *batizado* last year, when again, he'd been invited. He didn't want to be reminded of how he'd taken another woman to his bed just days before the very sad anniversary.

Now, two years after his first visit, he started wondering about Luna again. He had given her his card, but she never used it. What would he have done if she had? In the time since they'd been together, he'd spent his own time reconnecting with Capoeira and to a certain extent, reconnecting with himself. Slowly, he had begun to feel almost like his old self, a fact which his little sister, Delfina, was grateful for.

'I have missed you big brother,' she had said to him recently.

He gruffly replied, 'I have been right here.'

'No, you haven't.'

He had not argued her point as he knew exactly what she meant. He knew he had been gone for a while in all the ways that mattered.

He wondered what it would be like to bump into Luna again. Would he still feel intrigued by her? Would he still be inextricably drawn to her, to those eyes? He wondered what had gone on in her life since they'd met. Was she now with someone else? They'd had only one night together, but Luna Michaels had left an impression on him and had removed a chink in the armour that he'd constructed around himself since the death of his wife almost three years ago. Isabel was gone and so had the dream of the life they'd planned to have together. Their plans for a family and a future had been curtailed in an instant. He no longer had an interest in anything approaching what he and Isabel had shared. However, a part of him wanted to seek out Luna again and see if anything of the attraction they'd felt between them still lived.

When he arrived at the venue of the *batizado*, he had no problem finding his way around this time, though if he had bumped into Luna again in the hall, he would have definitely asked her for directions, as he'd done before, even if it was only in jest.

As it was two years ago, the Sports Centre was heaving with men and women dressed in the white uniform of their individual schools. He spotted some familiar faces. Some of whom he had met here back then or others he'd encountered in his travels around the Capoeira world. There was a wonderful energy in this room packed with capoeiristas.

'Javier, is that you? Sean told me you would join us this year.'

He turned around to see his friend Gabriela whom he'd first met two years ago in this very same place.

'*¡Amiga!*' He greeted her with a hug. '*¿Que tal?*'

'*Estoy contenta,*' Gabriela answered. 'Life is good.'

Javier could see the joy in her eyes. They had stayed in contact since they'd met here two years ago, the first *batizado* either of them had ever attended at this school.

'It's so good to see you,' he said.

They had become very close in that time. Though she was in London and he was in Spain, their friendship had flourished over more video calls than either of them could count. There were few people he had ever opened up to about what he had been going through after he'd lost his wife and Gabriela had been one of those few.

'And you too. Don't you owe me a bottle of wine from your winery? I've been dying to try it.'

'I've got some with me. I'm glad you'll finally be able to try it.'

'Me too.'

'Where's that husband of yours?'

'He'll be back in a minute. He's changing the baby.'

'Ah, *sí*. ¡*Carlito*! How is he?'

'He's a year old and a handful, but I wouldn't have it any other way.'

'It's always good to have Capoeira blessed by the presence of the new generation.'

Gabriela smiled. 'We have been blessed by two new babies at our school since you were last here. There's my Carlos, of course, and there's little Lexi. She's a sweetheart. Carlos and her are great playmates. Her mom should be bringing her today. We'll take turns to watch the babies so both of us new moms can have a turn doing the workshops and playing in the *roda*.'

'*Bueno*. I am so happy for you and Sean that you have your son. Children are a blessing,' Javier said.

'That they are,' she nodded in agreement. 'What about you? No little, '*Javiers*', running around?'

Javier laughed, though his laughter did hold a hint of remorse too. He and Isabel had never made it far enough to fulfil that particular dream.

'No, I have not been so blessed,' he said, sombreness in his tone.

Just then, Javier looked down and saw a little face looking up at him. It was a little girl, with the most curious eyes. Not only curious in the sense that she was looking at him in a way that might make you think she was working something out in her head, but also in the sense of the striking colour of said eyes. They were golden brown. He'd only ever seen that colour of eyes on one other individual in his entire life.

What are the chances?

He smiled at her and shook his head, clearing

away the thought of the coincidence.

Then he watched her run over to Gabriela, who was still in front of him, and started pulling the legs of her trousers.

'Cayi… Cayi…!' the little girl said.

Gabriela looked down. 'Lexi! You little escape artist!' Gabriela scooped her up into her arms. 'Where's your *Mamá*?'

Undeterred, the little girl demanded again, 'Cayi!'

'That's what she calls Carlos. Neither of them can quite get the other's name right yet. But they speak their own language.'

Gabriela smiled and bounced the little girl around on her hip.

'I wonder where her mother is,' Gabriela said as she scanned the room.

Once again, the little girl's attention had gone to Javier. Now that she was even closer to him, he had an even better view of her golden-brown eyes. They were striking. There was something else there, too which held his attention about the girl. It was the way she cocked her head as she looked him straight in the eyes. Then, she stretched out her arms to him.

'I see you've got a new admirer,' Gabriela said with a grin.

Little Lexi tried, even more, to reach out to Javier, so much so that she started to fuss as she wasn't getting her own way.

'Sorry Javier, I don't think she's going to calm down until she gets what she wants. Would you mind?' Gabriela held the little girl out to him.

'Of course.' Javier was happy to take her. He liked children and they'd always seemed to get along with him. Lexi eyed him with an even more intense stare. Then she touched his cheeks with her little chubby hands and gave them a little pat. She briefly turned her gaze back to Gabriela and giggled at her triumph. The next thing Javier knew, the little girl had rested her head on his shoulder.

'She must really like you! Do you have this effect on all the girls?'

Javier laughed. 'I can't say that I do.'

'Ah, there's her *Mamá* now.' Gabriela waved to someone behind Javier. 'Luna! We have your little Harriet Houdini right here.'

At the mention of the name of Lexi's *Mamá*, Javier's breathing stopped.

Surely, it could not be his Luna, right?

But even as he thought that, he already knew that the striking golden brown eyes on this child were too much of a coincidence.

'I believe she may one day give Houdini a run for his money,' Luna said with a laugh.

He hadn't yet turned around. But if he had any doubts as to if the mother of this child and his

Luna were one and the same, then those doubts were immediately squashed when he heard her voice from behind him.

Even as he was going into shock, now that he knew *his* Luna had a child, he could feel the slowed, even breaths of the little girl who still had her head on his shoulder. He could tell that she was now fast asleep.

Slowly, Javier turned around. He didn't know how it was possible that Luna would be even more beautiful than he remembered from two years ago. Their eye's met and held. In an instant, the dozens of occupants in the room disappeared, at least as far as Luna and Javier were concerned. Those eyes that, clearly, her daughter had inherited from her, glimmered. He watched as something resembling fear crossed her face before she composed herself again.

'Javi...'

He could see from her demeanour that she was shocked to see him there.

'It seems my new little friend here belongs to you, Luna,' he said.

'Y...yes, she does.' She still hadn't come any closer than a couple of metres.

'I think she's fast asleep,' he said.

Gabriela giggled, 'Anyway, I'll leave you to it. I need to go find Sean and my little rug rat. Lexi does seem to have made herself right at home in Javier's arms.' Then, Gabriela was gone.

'Yes, she certainly has.' Luna's face still looked a little like a deer in headlights.

'It's nice to see you again, Luna.'

'Same here.' Then she cleared her throat. 'Here, I'll take her.'

Javier slowly handed Lexi over to Luna, doing his best not to wake her as he did.

'Thank you for holding her,' she said as she rocked Lexi in her arms.

'She was no trouble, very pleasant actually.'

'She usually is.'

'So, you have a child now. A lot has changed.'

'Yes.'

'Is her father a capoeirista too?'

'Yes... he is.'

'Is he in the picture?' Javier thought being direct was always best. He had wondered if the old attraction he'd felt for Luna would still be there two years later. Without a shadow of a doubt, he could feel that there was still something between them. That she now had a child, did not scare him off. But if she were in a committed relationship, he would back off and respect that.

'N...not exactly.'

'So, you're a single parent then?'

'You could say that.'

Javier stroked Lexi's head of dark curls.

'She has your eyes,' he said, meeting her eyes. 'She's beautiful.'

'Thank you.'

'Why the name "*Lexi*"?'

'Because her real name sounds a bit too grown up for her right now. "*Lexi*" is short for "*Alejandra*".'

'*Alejandra*... You went for a Spanish name. Is her father Spanish speaking?'

'Yes.'

'Ah, that explains it. It seems you have a type.'

As he spoke, there was a part of him that was beginning to feel a little envious of the man Luna had cared about enough to let him give her a child. The thought shocked him.

'Apparently, I do.'

'OUTPLAYED' EXTRACT

Swipe to see an extract from
OUTPLAYED (Era Capoeira, Book 3)

CHAPTER 1

- ginga -

Dominic sat on the barstool nursing his second glass of bourbon. He was not having a good day. In fact, the week hadn't been anything to write home about either. The absolute last place he wanted to be tonight was out in public. He would have preferred to be alone in his apartment with nothing but a few more glasses of bourbon for company. If he'd had any other choice, he would have left already. But this was his lot in life tonight, so he just sat there and kept on sipping.

The bar was busy. He couldn't wait for them all to be gone. He had been sitting here on the short end of the 'L' shaped bar for almost an hour and had barely looked up since then. However, some invisible force was making him raise his gaze now.

There was a woman sitting at the bar a few metres away from him. She was staring straight ahead and Dominic thought she could probably see her reflection in the mirror behind the bar. Her back was straight, her neck was long and her skin looked like smooth milk chocolate. All his life, Dominic had always had a type, and this woman was definitely it.

The dark strappy top she wore showed off her elegant shoulders. He watched as she gracefully lifted her glass of white wine and planted red lips around the rim. She took a sip. He saw her chest rise and fall as she savoured the cold liquid making its way down her swan-like neck. It was at that moment that Dominic felt a stirring in his boxers.

Fuck! Where the hell did she come from?

He had been perfectly content in his misery and now this woman had come out of nowhere to make him horny.

For fuck sake!

Try as he might, he couldn't drag his eyes off of her. He watched as her jaw tightened and her lips pursed. He'd never seen the woman before in his life, but he would bet anything that she was in almost as bad a mood as he was in right now. Her gaze almost never left the back of the bar and she only looked down whenever she picked up her glass.

He was half tempted to get up, go over there and see if he could turn her frown upside down. He didn't do that, of course. She was hot, but his current mood made him unfit for human company.

So instead, he brought his gaze back down and took another sip of his bourbon. He didn't look up again until something in his peripheral vision pulled his attention again. It was a drunk. London on a Friday night heaved with them. There was nothing special about this one except one thing. He had placed himself on the stool next to the woman who was Dominic's type, as the seat had just been vacated by its previous occupant. The drunk was making eyes at her and his intentions were written all over his inebriated face. From what Dominic could see, the woman was paying the drunk zero attention. Then, he fully turned on his stool, faced her and started talking to her. Dominic wasn't close enough to hear what was being said, but he thought he could make a good guess.

The woman, as she was doing before, kept her gaze forward at all times. The drunk clearly didn't appreciate that, so he tried another tactic. Dominic watched him raise his index finger and place it on her arm, which had been resting on the bar. Without even turning her head to look at him, she took her free hand, lifted his offending finger and dropped it off to the side.

Dominic's eyes widened in shock. Never before had he seen someone react like that to being pestered by a drunk. This woman was clearly a smooth operator who was not easily flustered. His curiosity about her went up tenfold.

The drunk persevered. He lifted his arm and placed it around her shoulders. It was at that point that the woman spun smoothly the other way, away from the drunk and gracefully got to her feet, taking her glass of wine with her.

How did she move like that? Effortless!

The woman walked away from the bar and headed in the direction of the large fish tank in the corner. She continued to sip on her wine and this time, it was the fish in front of her that drew her gaze.

Lucky fish!

Now that she was standing, Dominic could see that she had very long, shapely legs and a svelte-like body. Her legs looked toned beneath the skin-tight dark trousers she wore. For the first time, he wondered why she was here alone, because she was most definitely here alone. No one expecting company acted like she did. Everything about her oozed sex appeal, from the way her shoulder length hair framed her beautiful face, to the perfect curve of her tight arse and the graceful way she poured that wine down her throat. Once again, Dominic felt his groin come to life.

It seemed the woman had acquired something of a stalker. The drunk, unperturbed by her previous blow off, walked over to where she now was on his unsteady feet. It was at this point that Dominic realised that he might have to take a short break from his barstool of misery and throw the guy out. The last thing he'd wanted tonight was to interact with any member of the public, but his conscience would never let him just sit there while someone was being harassed. In the mood he was in, however, the drunk had better pray that Dominic would be able to control himself if he made him have to get up off of his stool.

The drunk went straight up to her and grabbed her arse with one of his filthy hands. She spun around on instinct and sloshed her drink all over the drunk. The woman's beautiful face screwed up in anger. He wasn't sure if she was more pissed that he dared put his hand on her or that he'd made her spill her drink. Either way, Dominic's near empty glass of bourbon was placed down on the bar as he swung around and placed one foot on the floor. He took a deep breath and was prepared to lift himself to his full six feet of height. Before he could though, he watched as the woman put her now empty glass on the tray of a passing waiter as she grabbed the drunk by the scruff of his shirt and pulled him in, closer to her. She towered over him. Her expression now grew menacing. She said something to him and then shoved him away. The drunk nearly fell over.

Dominic stilled his movement. He realised that she might not be in need of him after all. The sexy woman showed no fear as she appeared to threaten her pest. Dominic thought that surely that would be the end of it. The drunk had been given fair warning that she would not take his shit and he could go drown himself in another pint of beer, right?

Right?

When the man regained his balance after she'd shoved him, he had not learned his lesson. He instead launched himself at the woman and this time his face was furious. Without hesitation this time, Dominic rose to his feet, and thought that it was time he put an end to this. The situation looked like it was about to get out of hand. Dominic had spent his life training in a number of hand to hand combat skills, but he knew that he wouldn't need to employ even a fifth of them to get this piece of crap out of the bar.

He had barely taken two steps when he saw the drunk point his index finger at her. It was inches away from the woman's face.

'You fucking bitch!' the drunk sputtered loudly. 'Who the fuck do you think you are? You think you're too good for me?' He spat as he spoke and slurred his words. This drew the attention of a many of the other patrons in the bar.

She spoke then and though Dominic couldn't hear her as her voice was so low compared to the ambient noise of the bar, he could read her red lips.

'Yes.'

By Dominic's fifth and sixth steps, he watched in utter shock as the woman grabbed the drunk's arm and executed a series of movements. She twisted his wrist, which caused the man to wince in pain and then she brought the same arm around to his back and then pushed it upwards. She then brought her free arm around the drunk's neck and whispered something in his ear.

He had seen this move executed a number of times in Hollywood movies and also in some of his combat classes. But, he'd never before seen it performed by a sexy woman, with red lips, a long beautiful neck and a body to die for. It was clear that the woman was a lot more than she appeared.

She doesn't need me at all, does she?

Dominic froze on the spot. The wicked side of him wanted to see how this would play out. From his new vantage point, Dominic could see a tattoo on her upper arm. It was of a snake.

What is that? A python?

The woman pushed the man away from her one last time and was about to walk away. She clearly thought her work here was done. How wrong she was!

In one last ditch effort to prove that he was a 'man', the drunk came at her one last time.

'What a fucking c—'

He never got a chance to finish his disgusting expletive as she'd heard him coming. She glance over her shoulder and without turning around fully, she brought her bent right leg up and then launched kick straight at the drunk's chest. He looked stunned as he stumbled back.

Not just a pretty face, huh?

The drunk must have had a screw loose, because he came back for more. This would be the last, however. Within seconds, the drunk was flat out on the ground, inhaling the dust off of the floor. He showed no movement except for the occasional twitch.

How he'd ended up there was a sight to behold.

Dominic was proficient in a number of martial arts, including Jujitsu, Taekwondo and Krav Maga. He'd also dabbled in a few others. Without a shadow of a doubt, the way she'd just executed that spinning kick, which had landed the drunk flat out on his face, proved that she was a highly skilled fighter herself. The drunk had definitely barked up the wrong tree tonight.

Is it wrong that watching her drop that drunk turned me on?

Dominic spun back around to the bar and spoke to the bartender. 'Jamal, pour me another glass of whatever *she*,' Dominic indicated the woman, 'was having.'

Jamal nodded, picked up a bottle of Sauvignon Blanc and poured a glass. Dominic took it, walked over to where the drop dead gorgeous force-to-be-reckoned-with was still standing, stepping over the drunk on his way. He held the glass out to her. She was not as tall as him, but she was pretty darn tall for a woman.

'Here. I believe yours got spilt,' Dominic said.

The woman looked up and her beautiful dark brown eyes met his grey ones.

If he'd dropped down dead right now on the floor next to the drunk, Dominic would have thought his life was worth it. Observing her from across the bar had been enough to get turned on. Now, standing inches away from her, his groin went into overdrive. He was glad that the lighting in the bar was low and that his trousers were black.

Without a word, she took the glass from him and brought it to her red lips. Even as she sipped, she did not take her eyes off of his.

Fuck me! I've died and gone to heaven!

She lowered the glass but not her eyes. 'Thanks.'

Her voice was like silk. Dominic knew his hard on could not take it anymore, so he knew he had to be the one to look away first. He did the first thing that he could think of. He turned around and looked down at the drunk, still lying flat out on the floor. He pulled a walkie-talkie out of his back pocket, pressed the button on the side and spoke into it.

'Tony, where the hell are you?'

A crackling sound came through the device, followed by a reply. 'I'm just outside having a smoke.'

'You don't get paid to have a smoke in the middle of your shift. Get your arse in here. Now!' It was shit like this that really pissed Dominic off.

'Sure, Dom,' said Tony, a little fear coming across in his voice.

'Hurry up!' Dominic added. 'There's some trash in here that needs to be taken out.'

'Sure thing, boss.'

Dominic placed the device back into his pocket. Then he turned back to the woman still standing behind him, sipping on her white wine.

'You alright?' Dominic asked.

She nodded, a smirk forming on her lips.

'Where did you learn that kick? Karate? Muay Thai?'

The woman's eyebrow rose. 'Capoeira.'

'Ahh...'

Colour me impressed!

Dominic took the opportunity, being this close to her finally and put it to good use. Her face was perfect. He loved her bone structure. All he wanted to do was run his finger along her cheeks and down her long, swan-life neck. He didn't dare, however, as she'd probably try to drop him like she'd just done to the drunk.

Instead, he let his eyes do the touching, being careful not to let it look too obvious that he was memorising every inch of her body.

'Nice tattoo,' he said. 'What is it? A python?

She gave him a sly smile. Her eyes shun with mischief. 'No. A viper.'

BOOKS BY THIS AUTHOR

More Than Fire

Jasmine King is a successful actress living in London. She has everything going for her... career wise. In the love department, her life is a disaster area. After yet another failed relationship, she decides to take a long overdue trip back to the place she was born, Guyana.

What she doesn't count on was that the trip would force her to once again confront some long buried feelings she had for an old friend. Ten years should have been more than enough to put those emotions behind her. But what Jasmine quickly realises is that fate had other plans for her.

Stefan Hathaway was now a strikingly handsome man, with even more magnetism and charm than he had years ago. Women were still throwing themselves at him. Jasmine finds that not only is her old attraction still there, but it has exploded!

How will she navigate this predicament and not make a fool out of herself? Would Stefan still see her as one of the guys? Is finding out if there could be more between them this time, really worth risking their friendship?

'MORE THAN FRIENDS' REVIEWS

Amy, Amazon UK Review (25 Oct, 2022)

★★★★★

Sizzling and sexy

This is a sizzler! Jasmine and Stefan's will-they won't they romance is packed with friendship, fun, laughter, TV glamour, beautiful scenery and H.O.T. chemistry between the leads. This is a smoking hot tale of love (and lust) that makes you want to jump on a plane to Guyana and hang out with these characters. Stefan, the smouldering male lead, is a tortured soul - can Jasmine save him? Great read - highly recommend.

Di Kecap, Amazon US Review (11 Oct, 2022)

★★★★★

heartwarming

Watching the story unfold was heart warming,

comical, heart wrenching, frustrating, sexy, uplifting, but most of all one of the sweetest love stories I've read this year. I must admit I loved every minute of More Than Friends.

Manisha, Amazon U.S. review (5 Oct, 2022)
★★★★
Friends to Lovers
This is the first time reading from this author and the storyline is good and the characters are great.

Sarah, Goodreads review (20 Sept, 2022)
★★★★★
This is one of the best books I've read, and only read a couple this year, but love reading so going to try to read more before this year ends, this one is probably going to be #1 (best read of the year). Do not postpone this one, it's only a short book, 239 pages I think, but to anyone who loves contemporary romance, or best friends to lovers, pick this book up.

THE PLAYLIIST

@shoneljacksonauthor

Listen to the playlist
for 'Let's Play'.

www.ingramcontent.com/pod-product-compliance
Lightning Source LLC
La Vergne TN
LVHW010053170826
845678LV00012B/2125

* 9 7 8 1 7 3 9 2 5 2 1 1 3 *